VENOM

USA TODAY BESTSELLING AUTHOR
C.J. PINARD

*Crosby —
Beware of werewolves!*

C.J.

This book is an original publication of Pinard House Publishing.

This is a work of fiction. The names, characters, places, and incidents are products of the writer's imagination or have been used fictitiously and are not to be construed as real. Any resemblance to persons, living or dead, actual events, locales, or organizations is entirely coincidental.

Copyright © 2022 Pinard House Publishing, LLC

This is licensed for your personal enjoyment only. No part of this book may be reproduced, scanned, or distributed in any printed or electronic format without permission. Please do not participate in, or encourage, piracy of copyrighted materials in violation of the author's rights. Purchase only authorized editions. All rights reserved.

PRINTED IN THE UNITED STATES OF AMERICA

ISBN: 9798425763099

PINARD HOUSE
PUBLISHING

ACKNOWLEDGEMENTS

Cover Art by Kellie Dennis at Book Cover by Design

Photograph: Golden Czermak @ Furious Fotog

Cover Model: Lovett Taylor

Copyediting by Amabel Daniels

Photo used with exclusive permission.

NIGHTHAWKS MC SERIES
Viper

Shadow

Phoenix

Venom

Face

"The more hidden the venom, the more dangerous it is."

~Margaret of Valois

1

OCEAN DEPOSIT

I could taste the beach air before actually seeing the ocean. I pushed the throttle on my bike and caught up with Phoenix, who was slightly ahead of me. I pointed to the sign indicating the next offramp and he acknowledged me with a nod.

Glancing at the impending sunrise ahead, I quickly checked my watch to see the sun would be up in all its glory in about an hour. As we exited the highway, I went ahead of him and drove into a rest stop. A few campers were parked around the lot but no people, being it was so early. I pulled into one of the spots and killed the engine as I waited for Phoenix to do the same.

We never bothered with helmets, so I raked my fingers through my hair as he put the kickstand down.

"What's up?" Phoenix asked, also smoothing down his wind-whipped red hair.

"Sun's up in about an hour," I said.

He nodded. "Yes, I know. You wanna stop here or ride another hour?"

It must seriously suck to be a vampire. Blood as a diet and the sun your worst enemy. I cared for this group of vampires, though, they'd given me a family when I had none. Phoenix—Gabriel—in particular, was who I was closest with. We went way back before I'd joined the Nighthawks.

"It's entirely up to you."

"I think we'll be okay, it's kinda cloudy this morning, anyway. I think we can make it to Jacksonville in an hour if we put the pedal to the metal."

I dismounted my bike. "Cool, let me take a leak and then we'll head over there."

"Take your time, man."

I wandered into the humid men's room of this dirty rest stop and wondered why I didn't just take care of this once we got to Jacksonville. But we'd been riding all night and I did have to go pretty badly, been holding it for miles. Vampires didn't have to use the bathroom and I didn't want to have to keep stopping for this. I was, however, very hungry, so Gabe was going to have to deal with me needing to find breakfast once we got there.

We quickly hopped back on the road and made it there before sunrise. After checking into a hotel for the day, I told Gabe I was going to get some food.

"Okay, I'll probably be out when you get back," he replied with a yawn.

I helped him put blankets over the window and, making sure I had the key card, I left the room and wandered downstairs. The hotel had a Starbucks in the lobby, so I ordered two meat and egg breakfast sandwiches and a decaf coffee, and sat alone while I ate them.

I was tired from being up all night, but that was nothing new. I had adapted to the vampires' sleep and wake schedule because I had to. And I didn't mind. It was no different than working the graveyard shift at the shipyard like I had for years. Even before that, I found myself working jobs that were at night and sleeping all day. I was pretty sure it was a wolf thing, anyway. We loved the night and the power we drew from the moon. With no romantic entanglements or relationships at all, I could keep these hours and do what I want, when I wanted.

"Why can't you get a normal job?" she screeched, throwing the wooden spoon at me. Spaghetti sauce flung all over the kitchen cabinets and me before it slapped me in the chest and plopped to the floor.

I stared at the object then back at her. "Are you done?"

"Oh, no, Harlan, I'm so far from being done. If you can't get a

regular job, with normal hours, then you should just get out."

I scrubbed my hand down my face, trying to steel my emotions. The full moon was approaching, and I was already on edge. "I have a regular job. I'm sorry you don't like the hours, but the pay is better if I work the warehouse on the graveyard shift."

"You do it to avoid me. I just know it. Use me for sex and to make your meals, and I get nothing in return," she snapped, narrowing her gaze at me.

"You know that's not true, now stop it." I was trying very hard not to lose it on this impossible woman.

"I can't do anything with you working those fucking hours and then sleeping all day. You expect me to plan this wedding all by myself?"

I honestly couldn't give two shits what colors we had or what the cake looked like. No way could I tell her that, though. "Amanda, listen. I have full faith in you. I'll go along with whatever you want. It's your day."

"No, it's our *day. And I can't do it all by myself!" She reached into the drawer and pulled out another spoon, angrily stirring the sauce.*

I picked up the dirty one from the floor, placed it into the sink, and tried to hug her, but she pushed me off. "Go away, Harlan."

I sighed and went into the bedroom. How was I going to tell her that I'd never have a "day job?" The shift was a perfect cover for the three nights a week I had to go romp around in the mountains as a beast controlled by the full moon. Fairly sure the inconvenience of my job's hours would pale in comparison to that if she ever found out.

I finished the sandwiches and shook my head to clear the memory. Relationships and me did not mix. Humans were out of the question since there was no way to explain my monthly full moon disruption, as I'd proved with Amanda. And female wolves were, well, batshit crazy—most of them, anyway. It was too late for me regardless. I was turning forty next year and didn't really see the point. I was getting too old for pups of my own and was starting to think I was just meant to be alone.

A terminal bachelor forever I'll be.

I woke before Gabe, brushed my teeth, and hopped in the shower. Once I was done, he was just waking up.

"Evening," I said, a towel around my waist, steam following me out of the small bathroom.

"How did you sleep?" he asked, getting up from his bed and stretching.

"So-so," I said. "Too close to the elevator, the dings kept me up."

He nodded. "I heard them too."

I jutted my chin at the bathroom. "It's all yours. I'm gonna head down and grab a coffee in the lobby. You want one?"

Gabe shook his head like I knew he would. "Nah, I'm good. I gotta find someone to eat before we head out though."

I chuckled. "Okay."

Once I got back up to the room with my plain black coffee, he was already showered and dressed. We'd decided since this wasn't a business trip, we'd leave the cuts and chains behind. Jeans and tees for us.

Gabe held up his phone. "Looks like the place is only about three miles from here. Let's take an Uber so we don't have to deal with anyone fucking with our bikes."

I lifted an eyebrow. "They could get fucked with here, though."

"True, but I trust them here parked by the front doors more than by the docks with less eyes on them."

"Okay. There are some people downstairs having 'happy hour', *regular job, with normal hours, then you should just get out."*

I scrubbed my hand down my face, trying to steel my emotions. The full moon was approaching, and I was already on edge. "I have a regular job. I'm sorry you don't like the hours, but the pay is better if I work the warehouse on the graveyard shift."

"You do it to avoid me. I just know it. Use me for sex and to make your meals, and I get nothing in return," she snapped, narrowing her gaze at me.

"You know that's not true, now stop it." I was trying very hard not to lose it on this impossible woman.

"I can't do anything with you working those fucking hours and then sleeping all day. You expect me to plan this wedding all by myself?"

I honestly couldn't give two shits what colors we had or what the cake looked like. No way could I tell her that, though. "Amanda, listen. I have full faith in you. I'll go along with whatever you want. It's your day."

"No, it's our *day.* And I can't do it all by myself!" She reached into the drawer and pulled out another spoon, angrily stirring the sauce.

I picked up the dirty one from the floor, placed it into the sink, and tried to hug her, but she pushed me off. "Go away, Harlan."

I sighed and went into the bedroom. How was I going to tell her that I'd never have a "day job?" The shift was a perfect cover for the three nights a week I had to go romp around in the mountains as a beast controlled by the full moon. Fairly sure the inconvenience of my job's hours would pale in comparison to that if she ever found out.

I finished the sandwiches and shook my head to clear the memory. Relationships and me did not mix. Humans were out of the question since there was no way to explain my monthly full moon disruption, as I'd proved with Amanda. And female wolves were, well, batshit crazy—most of them, anyway. It was too late for me regardless. I was turning forty next year and didn't really see the point. I was getting too old for pups of my own and was starting to think I was just meant to be alone.

A terminal bachelor forever I'll be.

I woke before Gabe, brushed my teeth, and hopped in the shower. Once I was done, he was just waking up.

"Evening," I said, a towel around my waist, steam following me out of the small bathroom.

"How did you sleep?" he asked, getting up from his bed and stretching.

"So-so," I said. "Too close to the elevator, the dings kept me up."

He nodded. "I heard them too."

I jutted my chin at the bathroom. "It's all yours. I'm gonna head down and grab a coffee in the lobby. You want one?"

Gabe shook his head like I knew he would. "Nah, I'm good. I gotta find someone to eat before we head out though."

I chuckled. "Okay."

Once I got back up to the room with my plain black coffee, he was already showered and dressed. We'd decided since this wasn't a business trip, we'd leave the cuts and chains behind. Jeans and tees for us.

Gabe held up his phone. "Looks like the place is only about three miles from here. Let's take an Uber so we don't have to deal with anyone fucking with our bikes."

I lifted an eyebrow. "They could get fucked with here, though."

"True, but I trust them here parked by the front doors more than by the docks with less eyes on them."

"Okay. There are some people downstairs having 'happy hour', so maybe you can get in a quick bite before we leave."

"Thanks," he said, grabbing the keycard and putting it into his wallet before leaving the room.

Normally, the guys paid for blood from willing donors, but in a strange town, I assumed he'd have to do that hypnotism shit on someone. The people downstairs were already pretty intoxicated on the free wine and beer the hotel handed out between 5 and 7 p.m.—so the sign had read.

I pulled up the car service app on my phone and saw the ride would be here in ten minutes. I shot off a quick text to Phoenix to let him know then checked the reservation in my email to make sure I had it ready for when we arrived.

When I got down to the lobby, I saw happy hour was still in full swing, so I took advantage by grabbing a few finger sandwiches and a beer. I sipped on it while looking around for Gabe. I quickly spotted him leaving the restroom area with a woman who looked happy and punch-drunk on vampire pheromones. With my keen eyesight, I saw two healing wounds on her neck.

He noticed me right away and I jutted my thumb toward the front door, just as I got a text that our car was out front.

The ride there was quick, and I wished I could see the ocean in all its sunlit glory, but the city lights and the half moon reflecting off the water was what I got instead.

After I tipped the driver, he left, and I pointed to the small shack at the end of the dock reading *Fishing Rentals*.

"I guess I should have asked this before we left, but do you have it?" I asked as we walked toward the shack.

Gabe pulled the pendant out of his front pocket and held it up by its leather strap. A witch had used it to curse him to a 150-year mortal sleep and then his girlfriend had been kidnapped by the witch's daughter last month in order to barter to get it back. The thing was dark, dangerous, and indestructible. It also gave me seriously creepy vibes and I just wanted it out of my presence.

"Good, let's get this over with."

We reached the rental shack, and I showed the guy working inside the boat reservation on my phone. He led us to a small speed boat and asked if we knew how to drive one.

"Yes, I've driven this type several times," I assured the man.

He handed me the keys. "Poles and bait are onboard, all ready for you."

"Thanks," I replied as we climbed aboard.

The first thing I'd done when I'd moved to the South from Colorado was go fishing. I loved the water and especially enjoyed being alone out on the lake or river all day trying to catch a fish. I'd done some ice fishing back home, but those were small row boats, nothing like this beast.

I put the key in and started the engine. "Sit and hold on, the first thrust will knock you on your ass."

"That's what she said, mmph!" he teased, making a thrusting motion with his hips.

I chuckled, purposely pushing the throttle full force before he was completely seated just so I could laugh at the big oaf falling. Unfortunately for me, his vampire reflexes had him seated before he could fall.

I yelled over the sound of the waves as we sped deeper across the Atlantic Ocean under a starry night sky. "Tell me again why you couldn't just dump that fucking thing in the Mississippi?"

"What if it washed up on shore?" he replied, still holding the cursed thing in his fist. "The bitch would have found it. It seems like this piece of shit has a mind of its own."

"Then you better not call it a piece of shit. It might crawl out of the ocean and find you!" I teased.

"True. Even for as much as it's worth, I still don't want it. I'd rather it be lost forever."

BSI Agent Bishop had done some research for him as a favor, and told Gabe it was worth thousands and thousands of dollars by the stone alone, combined with how old it was.

When we were a good mile out to sea, I slowed the boat down and killed the engine. Once we were calmly bobbing on the water, I got up and said, "Well, do what you came here to do."

Gabe nodded and looked down once more at the pendant. He ran his thumb over the giant opal stone and stared at it. He then wrapped the strap around the metal and stone and tucked it in so it wouldn't come loose. He lifted his arm, and, with vampire strength, he chucked it as far away from the boat as he could, like a seasoned baseball pitcher. We both watched as it flew so far it drifted from our eyesight, seeming to disappear into the vast nothingness of the ocean.

"Well, that was anti-climactic," Gabe said, shrugging.

"That's what your girlfriend said, mmgh!" I thrusted my hips like he had.

He laughed. "Nope, never."

I laughed too, patting him on his shoulder. "Let's go get a drink."

7

2
BAYOU WOLVES

We arrived back at the Nighthawks' clubhouse very early the next morning after having that drink and then checking out of the hotel and driving all night. We'd told the guy at the boat rental that we had a family emergency and had to leave, hence not catching any fish. Boy, how I'd have loved to have caught one or two, brought it back here, and cooked it up. I could only imagine the whining and complaining of the smell from everyone who lived here. I chuckled to myself at the thought.

"What's so funny?"

I turned to see Shadow standing at the doorway to the breakroom where I was heating up some leftovers I'd brought back from a Chinese place a couple days ago.

I lifted the food from the microwave and sat down. "Oh, nothing."

Shadow made a face at my food, and I was really getting tired of it. I didn't make comments or faces when they sucked on blood bags. I would occasionally razz them about it but not constantly. Everyone had to eat. They couldn't picture having to eat food and I couldn't fathom needing blood to survive. I'd tasted blood plenty, mostly in my wolf form, and was not a fan.

"Church in ten," he said.

I held up my cell phone. "Yep, I got the text too."

He took one last look at my food and left without another word. Usually, he was friendlier than that, so I had to wonder if something serious was going on.

After wolfing down my food – ha – I wandered over to the Cobalt Room for church before the club opened.

I stood at the front of the room with Viper, along with Shadow, Phoenix, Face, and Kovah. As all the prospects and other club members gathered inside, I looked curiously at a new face.

Viper pounded the gavel and the room quietened down. "I have two announcements tonight, so grab a drink if you don't already have one." He took a sip of his bloody wine mixture from a wine glass then set it down. "First, we have a new prospect. His name is Andy. Andy, will you please stand and tell us a little about yourself."

I recognized the newcomer as Phoenix's friend from the restaurant last month when we were celebrating the twins' mother making a full recovery from MS with the use of vampire blood and a little magic.

"Hi, I'm Andrew Jones, I'm about a hundred and eighty years old. Was born in the United Kingdom, then came to America when I was five."

I could hear a slight accent as he spoke, as if it was once strong and he was fighting to sound more American.

"I fought in the Civil War with my good friend Gabe here. I'm sorry—Phoenix. We fought, died, and were turned together. I've mostly been moving around from city to city every twenty years or so since then. While living in Texas, I met my fiancée Amber online and she lived here in New Orleans, so I moved out here about six months ago. I've lived here before, in the mid-1800s before Gabe went missin' on me." He grinned at his friend. "I'm glad to be a part of your club and look forward to learning all about it."

"Well, welcome, Andy." Viper looked at the rest of us. "Andy here has a law degree and license to practice and is apparently a pretty kickass at both criminal and real estate law, so his knowledge and certifications will be put to good use. He's just what I've been needing for the club. Damn sharks been draining me at 500 an hour for any little thing."

"Hey, you're still gonna be payin' me," Andy came back. "You'll just get the Nighthawks discount." He grinned.

"What's his club name, boss?" Dash asked from behind the bar where he was stocking bottles as he listened.

"We haven't decided yet," Viper said. "I'm up for suggestions." It was then I noticed Andy wore a plain black vest with no name patch.

"How about Badass?" Andy came back, putting on his most charming smile and lifting his arm into a muscle man pose.

"How about no?" Phoenix said, biting back a grin.

Andy flipped him off, laughing.

Viper shook his head. "Second order of business: The Bayou Wolves are requesting an audience with us," he said, reverting to boss mode.

"For what?" Kovah asked.

"They, apparently, need help with some human hunters."

Fuck. It must be bad if they were asking for our help. From the brief meeting I'd had with them last month, they seemed like a strong, proud group of wolves. I couldn't wait to hear what they had to say.

We had agreed to meet them in a neutral location. I still didn't know where their clubhouse was, but I was going to find out. Something about the Bayou Wolves intrigued me and it didn't take a shrink to figure out why.

I looked around the abandoned warehouse and thought it was pretty cliché to meet here, but it worked. Psycho, who seemed to be their club leader, stood against the back wall of the warehouse with his arms folded across his cut. He was a huge fucker. Three more big-ass wolves wearing cuts flanked him.

"Thanks for meeting with us. Normally, we just handle shit like this ourselves, but this fuckery is getting out of hand," Psycho said.

"Explain what's going on," Viper urged.

"We've lost two prospects and one family member so far to these assholes. They got their hands on some wolfsbane and have managed to shoot up wolves with it. Once they're down, these hunters are cutting out their hearts."

"In wolf form or human?" I asked.

Psycho measured me with a hard stare before answering, "Human. I truly don't think they have the balls to try to take on a wolf—tranqs or not."

"Agreed," I said, even though I wasn't really that confident. I'd been around human hunters before. Most of them were psychopaths.

"Do we have an ID on them?" Viper asked.

Psycho shook his head. "Only photos." He nodded to the guy next to him, whose patch read *Demon*, and grabbed the tablet from him after he'd tapped the screen. Psycho held up the electronic tablet. "The old lady of one of the prospects who was killed by these pigs was there when it happened. They attacked them down by the riverfront and she got a good look at them. Saw them a few days later and took these."

The photos showed three men eating in a restaurant during the day, and then of them walking down the sidewalk seemingly after they'd left the restaurant.

"Why didn't they kill her, too?" Kovah asked.

"Because she's human. They did threaten her though, to stay away from the Bayou Wolves and all wolves and shifters in general. She's under our protection now."

See? Stupid to get into a relationship with a human. Poor woman could have been killed.

Psycho continued, "She was smart to snap these and then hand them over to us, so now we're trying to handle it. But they haven't been spotted since."

"Can I get those sent over? I have some new software I could try to identify them with," Face said.

Psycho handed the tablet back to Demon and nodded. "Yes, get him your info."

"And you've done nothing to antagonize or otherwise threaten these hunters for them to just go around killing wolves?" Shadow asked.

Psycho narrowed his eyes at the giant. "No."

"So… if we identify them, you want them killed on the spot, then?" Viper asked.

"The endgame is death, but we'd like to chat with them first, make sure they don't have any more hunters out there lurking in the shadows. Basically, they're wanted dead or alive, but preferably alive."

Viper nodded. "Understood."

"So, you'll work with us on this?" Psycho asked.

"Yeah. I'm sure if they know of the existence of our kind, then they've got it out for us, as well. Human hunters have long been a problem over the years, which I will never understand. They may get a pot-shot in every once in a while, but they almost always end up dead by those they hunt," Viper replied.

I agreed. I'd seen a few over my lifetime too and it never ended well for them—ever. Why would a fragile human take on monsters that were faster and stronger than them?

"They're cocky little fucks with balls of steel," Psycho replied. "They only got to Donny and Paxton because of the wolfsbane. I need to find out where they got that shit from, as well."

"Probably a witch in the Quarter," I commented.

Well, just not Maria, she'd threatened to spray Phoenix and me with holy water. I bit back a grin at the memory. If she had wolfsbane, she surely would have threatened me with it.

He looked at me and said, "Can you find out who?"

I nodded and pointed to myself and the other Nighthawks. "We can sure try. No sane witch would sell me some, though. However, they may sell to a vamp."

"While we're here, I have a question," Viper said.

"Go ahead," Psycho grunted.

"How long have the Bayou Wolves been in New Orleans? We've been here ten years, hadn't heard of you at all until a couple weeks ago with the incident at Zombies."

"We're newly formed. I had a club back home in Minnesota. Moved down here last year and started a new one with a couple buddies."

Viper nodded. "That answers my question. Please know the Nighthawks don't consider anyone enemies until we feel threatened. You guys seem to be on the up and up, but there have been plenty of packs around here who've preyed on and killed humans. Last year, a pack kidnapped and tried to force the woman who's now my wife to marry into the pack and breed for them. We rescued her, but we'll not stand any of that here in New Orleans. You dig?"

Psycho's face turned red, and I watched as one of his fists balled. "Who are these wolves? We'll take care of them immediately. We don't fucking get down like that. Period."

"Oh, they were all wiped out, trust us. Haven't heard a peep from any of the chicks we left behind, either," Shadow replied.

"You killed the men and left the women?" he asked, looking from Shadow to Viper.

"Yes, we couldn't tell which were human or wolf in the midst of the chaos. We knew most of the men had to be wolves, so we just got rid of them all," he replied.

Demon looked at Psycho. "We would have done the same thing if they were vamps, boss."

Psycho nodded slowly. "Well, you ain't gonna have to worry

about that with us around. We police our own and have zero tolerance for any kind of unnecessary kidnapping. We don't put up with rapes or attacking women or any of that type of shit either."

"Good to know. I look forward to working together to keep the peace here in New Orleans," Viper reiterated.

I watched Face approach Demon with his tablet, and they exchanged information. Then we left the abandoned warehouse. Guessed they didn't trust us enough yet to show us their clubhouse.

Not that I blamed them.

3

SHIFTING FAMILY

Boulder, Colorado – 2001

My body was burning up, and the icy mountain wind was a welcome reprieve. I stopped, closed my eyes, and let the wind cool me off.

"Don't stop, Harlan! We gotta beat him to the top!"

I looked over to see my cousin, Aaron, staring at me with crystal-blue eyes. The wind whipped his white fur around in circles.

"I know. Just trying to not overheat here. I'm burning up," I replied.

"You won't overheat, I promise. Just keep moving. We can rest when we get there. I can't let Jeramy best me again! I'll never live it down!"

I had a love-hate relationship with wolf telepathy. It was obviously very handy since wolves couldn't speak through their mouths except for a few woofs, barks, and whines. But it subjected me to stuff in my packs' heads that I *so* did not want to hear sometimes.

But he was right about Jeramy. That shithead was as competitive as they came, and he couldn't stand to let anyone beat him in a race.

I picked up the pace, the wind gliding over my black fur as I raced behind Aaron. Jeramy was his older brother, and they were constantly in competition for everything—their parents' affection, physical strength, and, of course, girls.

I was only nineteen and was still getting used to being a wolf. I'd known that on my eighteenth birthday I'd be turning—I grew up spending three nights every month babysitting my two younger brothers while my folks roamed the mountains—but nothing they explained to me ever prepared me for that first shift. I was the oldest of three, so I had to endure it first. Robbie and Jordan were in their mid-teens and were anxious and excited to become wolves. They had no idea the hell they were in for, but I just kept my mouth shut when they'd talk about it at the dinner table. They were going to have to find out the hard way like I did, that it was nothing like the movies. Wolves weren't heroes and badasses. We were the fucking villains.

"Yes!" Aaron yelled as he reached the peak of the mountain mere seconds before Jeramy.

We were belly-deep in snow, but it felt good, refreshing. I panted, trying to catch my breath.

"You guys are fucking cheaters!" Jeramy snapped.

I looked at my older cousin. *"How did we cheat? We're just faster than you."*

Of course, he didn't answer because he didn't have one. He just hated to lose.

"Let's find some food. I'm starving," Jeramy replied instead.

I agreed.

The first time I'd eaten a raw rabbit I thought I'd be disgusted, but it hadn't bothered me at all. I looked over to see Jeramy and Aaron standing stock-still, their eyes zeroed in on something. I slowly swung my gaze in that direction to see a small deer grazing nearby.

"On my count," Jeramy said. He sort of whispered it, too, which was hilarious, considering.

On three, we pounced. The deer was quick as she scampered away, but she was no match for three wolves.

Once we'd gotten our fill, we rested in the snow and cleaned ourselves up with our tongues. I looked around and saw dark spatters on the snow that sparkled under the full moon. I didn't need to see in color to know it was the doe's blood. I lapped up the snow as it turned to liquid in my mouth to wash down the rest of the deer's flesh.

Being in this form, we didn't have much to do. I had fretted before my first turn, wondering how I was going to entertain myself. I used to watch our family dog just sit and stare at us for hours and wondered what went through his mind. Didn't he get bored with nothing to do? Sometimes he would watch television but I wasn't sure how much of it he actually understood.

Once I turned, I realized my attention span was pretty short. If a woodland creature happened by, we could chase it for hours. Hunt it. Like a game. Sometimes I wrestled with my cousins and that helped pass the time.

We were just relaxing now. The trek up the steep mountainside had been pretty taxing, and now with full bellies, it was naptime. I closed my eyes and hoped I'd wake before morning came. Waking up naked in human form in a foot of snow was no fun at all.

"Get your hands off of her!" I yelled, yanking my dad's arm before he swung the belt once more to my mother's back. I pulled the belt from his fist and threw it to the ground.

He punched me in the jaw, sending my head rocking back with a snap. "Don't you fucking touch me, boy, or you're next!"

I rubbed my jaw and looked over to see my two younger brothers hunkered down with fear in their eyes as they watched from the dining room doorway. "Go to your rooms," I mouthed at them, making a shooing motion with my hand.

A piercing pain ripped through me, and I turned around to see my dad with the belt in his hand once more, the buckle ripping open the skin on my back. I felt warm blood trickle down the length of my spine.

My mother sat cowering in the corner, crying. As long as he wasn't hitting her, I'd take the whooping. One day I'd be bigger than him, and he would pay the price.

I jerked awake with a start as my cousins woke me to begin our descent down the mountain before morning came and we were human once more. The mountain I wished some days I could just live on and not have to go back home.

Grateful the full moon was behind me for the month, I finished getting ready in the small bathroom I shared with my brothers. I had a job interview lined up for a large warehouse a couple of towns over that distributed vehicle parts. I was desperate to move out of my parents' house, but the part-time job I'd been working at the movie theater since high school was not going to cut it. I hated the job almost as much as I hated my home life.

I hopped into my old Ford pickup, and it didn't take long to arrive at the warehouse. I waited in the small reception area in front of a cute receptionist who kept glancing up at me through her lashes. I smiled back at her politely.

She said, "Mr. Henderson will be out shortly. He's doing another interview right now."

"Thanks for letting me know," was all I could think to reply.

I had exactly zero experience with women. I never had a high school girlfriend, nor did I have any sisters. I did not know how to talk to them, so I mostly stayed to myself.

"So, if you get hired, will this be your first job?"

I looked up from the *Field & Stream* magazine I'd been thumbing through and stared at the receptionist. She had hopeful blue eyes and wore her brown hair in a ponytail. She was average-looking but pretty. Clearing my throat, I said, "No, I have one now, just need a better paying one."

"Oh yeah? Where's that?" she asked, blowing a big bubble of

pink gum.

"The movie theater in Boulder."

Why was I even telling this chick my business?

"Oh, nice. I love going to the movies." She smiled at me.

"Well, if you worked there, you'd hate it."

"I bet you get to see all the movies for free, huh?" she asked, now with her hand under her chin like this conversation was the most interesting thing about her day. And it probably was.

"We'll be in touch, Mr. Smith."

We both looked over to see a tall man in a suit shaking a young man's hand before he exited the office. The man then looked down at his clipboard, then back to me. "Mr. Lahey, I presume?"

I stood and shook his hand. "Yes, sir."

"I'm Dan Henderson, I'll take you back."

"Good luck," the receptionist said, wiggling her fingers at me in a wave.

I smiled politely and cleared my throat nervously.

Dan must have caught on because he chuckled. "I see you met Amanda. Hope she didn't yap your ear off while you were waiting. I hired her because of her friendly, outgoing personality. But she can come on a bit… nosy, if you catch my drift." He looked at me.

And here I thought she was flirting with me.

"She wasn't a bother, sir. Nice girl."

"Well, good. Let's get on with the interview."

After a few minutes and some pretty easy questions, he walked me out to the reception area and said the same thing he'd told that Smith guy, that he'd be in touch.

Before I left the office, I heard, "Bye, Harlan. Enjoy the rest of your day."

I turned around to see Amanda wink at me. My face turned red, and I cleared my throat again, forcing a smile. "You too, Amanda."

As I drove home, I kept obsessively going over the interview in my mind. Had I said the right thing? Did I mess up any of my answers? Did I look into Dan's eyes with confidence as I spoke like my mom had told me to?

Pretty soon, I was home, and Mom immediately wanted to know how it went.

"Fine, just fine," I assured her.

"Are you really going to move out if you get that job?" she asked, turning to look at me from where she was scrubbing the inside of the oven wearing yellow cleaning gloves. She wore a blue short-sleeved shirt, and I could see the finger-shaped bruises on her upper arm still healing. She caught me staring and pulled the sleeve down lower, as if that could hide the evidence of my father's violence.

"You need to leave him," I said for the hundredth time through gritted teeth.

She ignored that and asked again, "Are you really gonna move out, baby?"

I shrugged as if I didn't know, but I already knew the answer. I didn't understand why she seemed sad about me moving. Dad constantly complained about the grocery bill, and with one less mouth to feed, wouldn't that be a good thing for them? I was nineteen, no need to still be living at home. My little brothers were enough of a handful. A part of me wondered if she was scared to let me move out, for fear of what Dad would do to her once I wasn't there.

"I'll think about it," was my reply.

"Okay, but you always have a place here, you know," she replied, piercing me with her tired brown eyes, and then going back to her task.

"I know, Ma. I appreciate it. Love you." I kissed the top of her head before I went into my bedroom and closed the door. I was definitely out of here as soon as I'd saved up enough for a small apartment or mobile home. I craved independence and nothing was going to stop me. Besides, what girl would want to date me if I still lived and home with mommy and daddy? No thanks.

I thought about my little brothers and hoped they'd be all right once I left. If things got worse with our father, I'd just bring them all with me.

4

WOLFSBANE

Present Day

I plucked an apple from the basket on the counter in the breakroom, threw it up in the air, then caught it before polishing it on my shirt. Jemini and Gabe sat at the table drinking blood from mugs. Jemini's read, *I Want to Believe* with a picture of a green spaceship.

I fist-bumped Phoenix and then looked at Jemini. "Hey, girl."

She looked up at me and smiled. "Hi, Harlan."

"So… what might a vampire say if you invited him over for dinner?" I asked her.

Gabe groaned.

"What?" she asked, grinning behind the lip of the coffee mug.

"He'd say, 'No fangs, I just ate necks door!'" I used my first two fingers to pretend to plunge them into her neck.

She giggled.

Gabe shook his head. "That was terrible."

I bit into the apple and grinned at him as juice ran down my lips and into my beard. After I swallowed that bite, I said, "You loved it."

"Your jokes are ridiculous," Face said, walking in with a smile and sitting down at the table with us.

"So's your face," I quipped.

He nodded. "I know."

"Whatcha got?" I asked, pointing at the tablet he stared at.

He tapped some buttons on the screen and turned it around. "I already showed this to Viper and the others, but I got a match on one of the human hunters."

I looked at a mugshot of a young man with stubble on his chin and shaggy light-brown hair. He scowled at the camera while he held a "New Orleans PD" plaque in front of his chest. The numbered height indicator behind him showed him to be about five-foot-eleven.

"Lyle Manchester of River Ridge, Louisiana. Twenty-eight, three priors. Two DUIs, one B and E."

"What was the breaking and entering for?" I asked.

Face grinned. "Agatha's shop."

"Let me guess. He stole wolfsbane?" I asked dryly before taking another bite of the apple.

"It actually doesn't say if he stole anything," Face said.

"Wolfsbane isn't as easy to acquire as people think it is," said Bloome as she and Shadow walked into the breakroom. "It only grows in certain parts of the country, and then it has to be ground down and mixed with other herbs, not to mention some magic has to be performed on it as well."

"So, it's worth the risk to steal it," I stated.

She nodded. "Exactly. I tell you, if I was running a shop and had to go through all that work, I would charge an arm and a leg for it."

I looked at Phoenix. "Let's go down to Agatha's and see if she sells any."

"We can, but I doubt she'll tell us jack shit with you around." He looked at Jemini. "But she'd probably sell some to a sweet little vampire who's just lookin' for a little protection against the big, bad wolf." He lifted his voice to mimic a Southern belle.

Jemini laughed. "Okay, I'll do it. Let's go."

Phoenix and I waited on our bikes across the street from Agatha's. The plan was Jemini would inquire and then get pricing for the wolfsbane. She wasn't in there three minutes before she came out of the shop. She looked both ways down this one-way street before crossing it to us.

"It's a specialty-order item only. I tell her how much I want, she makes it up custom. The plant contains a toxin that's harmful to humans too, so it's got to be handled carefully. Then there's the process of liquefying it for putting into drinks or needles. It's a thousand dollars an ounce."

I whistled through my teeth. "Steep, but understandable. Aconite is the poison she's talking about it. Wolfsbane isn't the only so-called drug humans used to use it for. They put it in food to kill someone or, back in the day, on blades while in battle. It's nasty, nasty shit."

"Sounds like it," Gabe agreed. "What would it do to us?"

"Probably just give you a really bad day, but doubtful it'd kill you. Maybe stop your heart for a few minutes."

"Yikes," he replied, running a hand over his head.

"Let's go try a few more shops, see who else sells it in-shop or has it on special order," I suggested.

By the third store, the witches had obviously all communicated with each other, and the fourth shop was already expecting Jemini. The witch had told her she knew what she was up to, helping out the wolves, and asked her to leave, so we gave up. Guessed those witches were more loyal to each other than we thought. Seemed they'd be competing for business... but, apparently not.

"Gotta go report this to Viper so he can let Psycho and the

others know," I said as we headed back to the clubhouse.

Once we arrived inside, we found them at the Cobalt Room. We all squeezed into Viper's small office in the back.

"That's a steep price, but from what Bloome told me, it's a bitch to acquire and make," Viper said after hearing our report.

"It's not like you can just go down to the local nursery and buy a few plants," Bloome agreed. "Wolfsbane, or Monkshood, grows in mountainous regions, so they'd have to drive north until they reached the Smokeys to try to find some. I can see why it's so expensive."

"Where the hell did this Lyle character and his buddies get the money for this shit?" Viper asked.

"Who knows? Maybe he's got a deal with the witches," I said, knowing humans were resourceful and would do whatever they could for money when they wanted something badly enough. "Or he stole it."

Viper looked at Face. "Did you dig up anything on this guy that would indicate why he hates wolves?"

"The only suspicious thing is that his father was killed on a hunting trip when Lyle was thirteen. The kid was with him." Face looked up from the tablet and to us.

"Got the police report?" Viper asked.

Face began to read. "Park rangers reported finding the forty-six-year-old mauled to death by an animal. His son, Lyle, claims he was asleep in the tent when it attacked at approximately one-forty-two a.m. The child was awakened to Dad screaming for help, came out of the tent, but the animal was gone. Lyle used a satellite phone to call for help."

"Let me guess, full moon that night?" I asked.

Face looked at me then to the device. "Good question. Let me put the date into my moon calendar app."

"Wow, there's an app for everything," Phoenix grunted.

"Venom should have it on his phone," Face said without

looking up.

I shook my head. "I don't have it. I don't need it."

"That's a Nighthawks-issued phone. We all have the app," Face replied.

Guessed that showed how much I cared about the damn device. I only used it for calls and texts, to order food, and to check the time. I couldn't care less about social media or playing games like some of the other guys.

"Yes, November eighth of that year was a full moon," Face finally said.

"I'd bet money the kid did see a giant wolf, but didn't report it for fear of sounding crazy," Viper said.

"Coroner's report says it was most likely a bear or mountain lion."

"We don't have mountain lions in Louisiana," Shadow commented.

"They were hunting in Kentucky. Sorry, left that part out," Face said, chagrinned.

"We got an address for this fool?" Viper asked.

Face nodded with an eyeroll. "Of course, boss. Come on now." He rattled off a local address in River Ridge, a small, quiet suburb of New Orleans, and then sent it out over the group text.

"It's late, but we'll set up a round-the-clock stakeout of these guys." Viper looked at me. "Obviously, you'll be on the dayshift."

"Obviously," I said. "Me and Kovah."

I noticed the sunglassed fool was nowhere around. Must be with his wife.

"I'll let him know," Viper said. "We start tomorrow morning. I want to know this guy's every move."

"Why don't we just fuckin' kidnap him, boss?" Shadow asked.

"I thought about that, but we need to know who he hangs with. Who's gonna go reporting him missing if he does disappear,"

Viper replied.

He had a point. Normally, we didn't care, but the fact this hunter kept company with other hunters, we needed to make sure we eliminated the threats altogether.

I supposed I should probably try to get some sleep if I was going to have to be up all day. I went upstairs to my apartment and popped two melatonin and a small shooter of whiskey before lying down, hoping to get a couple hours' rest before I had to spend the whole day in a car with Kovah.

5

STAKEOUT

"If nothing else, it's nice to see the sun," Kovah remarked, jutting his chin at the sunrise.

"You're not wrong about that, brother," I said, gnawing on a toothpick after we'd just finished a few breakfast sandwiches from the local fast-food place.

We were in the white van and had parked across the street from the guy's house. Thankfully the van contained a stack of several different magnetic decals to choose from. Today, we were Crescent City Water District employees.

The house was small, older, and very average. It was 9 a.m. and so far, we hadn't seen anyone go in or out in the last two-and-a-half hours. I'd gotten about four hours of sleep and was going to need another coffee if I was gonna be able to stay awake. Stakeouts sucked.

"So, what do you and the wife do to stay awake during these boring-ass things?" I asked him, knowing his wife, a vampire, was also employed by the Justice Department and he went on a lot of stakeouts with her.

He grinned at me. "You really wanna know?"

I groaned. "On second thought, no."

He chuckled. "Get your mind out of the gutter, wolf-boy. It's mostly stupid games, like the license plate game, slug-bug, cloud shapes, you know, usual shit."

"So basically, you behave like twelve-year-olds," I said wryly.

He laughed. "Knock it all you want, it does help pass the time."

"I guess that's better than a card game or something," I said.

He nodded. "Yeah, I guess."

"How did you meet your wife, anyway?" I asked, desperate to keep the conversation going because I was bored out of my mind.

He glanced over at me, and I could see his freakish white eyes behind his sunglasses by the sun shining in through the window. "It's a long story."

I waved my hand in front of us. "I clearly have the time."

He sat up straighter. "Manta was working with the BSI. Well, she still does. At the time, she was investigating the Nighthawks. I helped her infiltrate the Shreveport clubhouse."

My eyebrows hit my hairline. "Infiltrate? Like, undercover?"

He teetered his hand from right to left. "Eh, sort of. They caught onto me pretty quick."

"And Viper didn't kill you?"

He nodded. "They almost did when they first caught me snooping around. Beat my ass pretty good. But after that, it was all good."

"So you went from trying to infiltrate them, to member?"

"Yup," he said, taking his sunglasses off and cleaning them with the hem of his T-shirt. He remained looking down as he continued. "I was practically begging to join when I found out they killed rogue vamps. It was all I did after I became this freak. It was my therapy." He pointed to his solid white eyes before replacing the sunglasses.

"Why did you hate vamps?"

"Succubus bitch did this to me. I've since calmed down and stopped killing every vamp in sight."

I chuckled. "You've obviously stopped killing vamps on sight, but you haven't calmed down. You got it bad for the succubuses."

"Succubi. Plural."

"Duly noted," I said, laughing. I'd seen him go Joker-esque

crazy when we came across one. His glee while killing one bordered on frightening and psychotic.

"And your wife, she likes working for the BSI?" I asked. I thought it would be pretty cool myself.

He nodded. "Yep. Except the moving around part, but it's par for the course."

"They make them move around a lot?"

"Yep. In fact, between me and you, bro, we're probably gonna be heading out within the next few months. They told her to choose a new spot and we've been trying to decide on a location."

My eyebrows shot up. "You're leaving the Nighthawks?"

He lifted a shoulder. "I kinda have to. I need to move with my wife. I mean, I won't leave-leave the Nighthawks, but I won't be able to be here anymore." He adjusted himself to face me fully. "You understand, right? I mean, I know you don't have an old lady, but once you do, you will."

I actually did understand and agreed with him. "I support your decision, Kovah. I mean, it's a hard spot to be in, and being that you both don't age, it's probably time to go. You been in this area a while, huh?"

"Yep, about twelve years," he replied.

"Well, thanks for leaving me to do all the daytime dirty work, you asshole," I said, grinning at him.

"Look," Kovah said, pointing across the street and shrinking down in his seat a little.

We watched as Lyle exited the house wearing khaki pants and a black polo shirt, a gold-colored emblem on the chest I couldn't quite read. He got into a small Toyota sedan and started it up.

"We gonna follow him in this thing?" he asked from the passenger's seat.

"That's what Viper wants," I said, shrugging as I started the van and put it in drive.

We trailed behind Lyle at a safe distance, and after about ten minutes, he drove into the city and parked in the employee lot of the Mercedes Benz Superdome, where he used a card of some kind to get through the electronic arm barring anyone else access.

He wandered out of sight as we sat with the van idling. "Guess we know where he works. Let's go back to the house and search it," I suggested.

"Sounds good to me," Kovah replied.

We arrived back at the house in River Ridge and waited a few more minutes before deciding to go in. With our clear eyesight and sharp hearing, we hadn't heard anything coming from the inside.

The back door's lock was easy enough to break, and once we were inside, we kept the lights off and used the sunlight through the window to see. The house was quiet with all the normal furniture in it, the fridge sparse with food. Two back bedrooms both held beds and dressers, but one had a large corkboard that took up most of the wall.

Kovah whistled under his breath as we both stopped short and stared at it. "Obsessed much?"

Full eight-by-ten photos of several of the Bayou Wolves peppered the corkboard, with strings wrapped around the tacks holding the photos in place. Each string was connected to another photo, and several newspaper articles were also pinned to the top. Three photos at the bottom, two men and one woman, had large red Xs through them, as if they'd been eliminated.

"We've lost two prospects and one family member so far to these assholes." Memories of what Psycho had said at our meeting echoed through my mind.

"Did we get photos of the two Bayou Wolves who'd been killed?" I asked absently.

"No," Kovah said, pulling out his cell phone and taking photos of the board and all its contents from several angles. "But I'm guessing it's these two." He pointed at the bottom photos of two males with the red Xs through them. "And who's the chick?" he asked.

"They said two prospects and a family member. That lady looks older. Maybe someone's mother," I suggested, shaking my head.

"That's fucked up," Kovah said, shaking his head as well and snapping a picture of her photograph.

I searched through drawers and the closet, not finding much. Certainly no secret vials of wolfsbane or receipts for large sums of money.

Kovah lifted the mattress and then looked under the bed. I helped him pull the dresser from the wall to make sure there were no holes or safes hidden there. We found nothing.

"Let's go look in the other room, maybe get a hint of who else lives here," I suggested.

We put everything back and left the door open as we'd found it before wandering into the other bedroom. It was dull, with just a bed and a dresser. Thankfully, a search of the closet yielded a large orange envelope with some documents and ID inside.

"I got a passport," I said after dumping the contents onto the unmade bed. "Leland Manchester, age thirty."

"Brothers," Kovah said, stating the obvious.

"Weird, the park ranger's report didn't mention this one as being on the hunting trip."

I nodded. "I agree. Why take a… thirteen-year-old and not the fifteen-year-old… if my math is correct."

Kovah took the passport from me, and I could see the wheels turning in his head. "Yep, he would have been fifteen then."

"Maybe he was still asleep when Lyle found the father? They obviously both hate wolves," I replied.

"It doesn't fucking matter," Kovah said, handing me back the passport. "Hold it open."

I did as instructed, and he snapped several photos of it before pocketing his phone. "Let's get the fuck outta here."

I replaced the passport back into the envelope, and after a quick search of the room, same as the other one, we found nothing. I put the envelope back into the closet, slid the doors closed, and we exited out the back door.

They would eventually notice the busted back door lock, but we couldn't care about that right now.

"You guys are awesome!" Face said, almost creaming his pants at all the info and photos we'd gleaned from our little stakeout.

I chuckled at his childlike excitement as he took his tablet and disappeared into the walkway that led to the clubhouse, no doubt so he could get on his computer and geek out.

"Now, we have the issue of the third hunter. We need to find out his identity ASAP," Viper said.

"I agree. I was thinking… maybe Psycho will let us interview the female witness?" I suggested.

"That's a good idea. Maybe she'll remember something," Shadow replied, lifting his bourbon to his lips and taking a swig.

The Cobalt Room wasn't very busy, but it was a Tuesday night. Just then, Ally approached and asked, "Y'all good with your drinks?"

"Yes, but any chance you could get me some tacos from the truck, sweetie?" I asked her.

"Beef, chicken, pork?" she asked, batting eyelashes at me.

"Whatever's on special, I'm not picky." I bit back a smile. I knew she had a thing for Fox, another prospect, so she was just being polite and not flirting.

She smiled. "Of course, Venom." She looked at Kovah. "You want some, as well?"

He nodded. "Yeah, tacos sound amazing."

She winked at us and went behind the bar, grabbed some cash from the drawer, and then wandered out the back door. The alley that flanked the club led straight to a line of food trucks. Shadow made a gagging sound. I flipped him off.

I lifted the beer to my mouth. "What did Psycho say when you gave him the information we've gotten so far?"

Viper set his bloody wine down and said, "I haven't told him yet. I wanted to present him with as much info as we had at once. Earn their trust and respect and all that shit."

I could see that. Psycho was a scary and tough wolf, but I got the vibe he'd have mad respect for us if we bestowed him with a shitload of information at once.

"Back to the female witness," Viper said. "I'll see if Psycho will let us talk with her."

"Do you think she'll talk to vampires, though?" Jemini chimed in.

I looked at her. "Why not?"

She shook her head. "Does she even know about us? And even if she does, doubtful she'd be comfortable enough."

"But you've never even met her," I argued.

She fixed me with that green stare I was sure made Gabe stop what he was doing and obey immediately, so I zipped my mouth shut with a nod.

"She's clearly comfortable around wolves, though," Viper said, grinning at me.

I honestly had no problem questioning this woman. I just didn't want to traumatize her any more than she'd already been. I couldn't wrap my brain around watching someone I loved having their heart cut out in front of my eyes. Witnessing abuse was traumatizing enough, which I had endured firsthand.

"I'll do it," I said. I looked at Viper. "Arrange the meeting and I'll be there."

BLOOD ON BLOOD

Longmont, Colorado – 2001

Six months into the warehouse job, I finally got up the nerve to ask Amanda out. As our initial meeting had been somewhat awkward, I'd finally loosened up from being around so many different personalities at this job. It also seemed that I'd grown another foot in height and put on about forty pounds due to the physical requirements of the job and my new obsession with the gym. We'd been dating about two months, and I was happy.

"Is it just me, or did you, like, get taller, since I first met you?" Amanda asked, her eyes wide as she shoveled a piece of popcorn in her mouth as we waited for the movie to start.

She hadn't been joking, she *loved* going to the movies.

"Well, judging by the growing pains, I would say so." Last month, I'd measured myself by marking on my wall at the top of my head with a pencil and then I used the tape measure. It showed 75 inches, so about six-foot-two. My dad was about that height, so it was no surprise I'd sprung up.

"Well, I think it's super sexy!" She blew me a kiss. Like a dork, I caught it and put it next to my heart. Then, she leaned in and pressed her lips to mine. I immediately began to get aroused, and her hand on my crotch didn't help. We were at the very top row of the theatre, and the movie about to play wasn't very popular, so the place was pretty empty with only a few people in it. She set the popcorn bucket on the seat next to her and then unzipped my pants, massaging me with her soft hand.

"Oh, God," I groaned.

The lights dimmed and the screen began to play previews, but I couldn't pay attention, especially when her mouth went straight onto my dick and began to suck. I grabbed her hair and hissed in pleasure. Of course, I barely lasted through one preview before I was shooting my load into her mouth.

She popped her head up out of my lap, looked around, and wiped her mouth with her finger. "Hmm, yummy."

After taking a swig of her soda, she resumed eating popcorn while I zipped up and fought taking a nap. After the movie, we went back to my new apartment, where we spent the rest of our Saturday afternoon having sex and watching bad reality TV before falling asleep.

My cordless phone ringing on my nightstand woke me out of a deep sleep. "Hello?" I answered groggily.

"Harlan, please come. Mom's in the hospital."

I sat up and scrubbed a hand over my face. "Jordan? What happened?"

He was quiet for a second before he said, "Dad."

"I'm going to fucking kill him," I growled, getting out of bed and sliding my pants on. "Which hospital?"

"Boulder Community. Come quick but please don't tell Dad I called you. Please."

"He's not going to have a head when I'm done with him," I snapped, ending the call.

"What's going on, Harlan?" Amanda asked groggily.

I pulled the Ford's key off my keyring and tossed it on the bed. "You can take the truck home. I gotta get to the hospital. My mom…"

"What happened?" she asked, sitting up and taking the sheet with her to cover her chest.

No way in hell was I going to tell her what a fucking bastard my dad was, so I shrugged. "Not sure, my brother just called. I'll call you later." I held up my flip phone before shoving it into my pocket.

"Love you," she said before flopping back down to the pillow.

I kissed her nose and sprinted out the door. I ran down the stairs and then took off on my new-to-me Kawasaki motorcycle I'd just bought. It needed some work, but it got me from point A to point B and it was fun learning how to work on it.

The fifteen-minute drive seemed to take forever. Once I reached the hospital, I parked in the first spot I found, killed the engine, and sprinted inside, forgoing the elevator and taking the stairs two at a time to room 412 where Jordan told me she was.

I swore as I entered the room. I wasn't prepared for what I saw: Her face was black and blue, one eye swollen shut. Her left ear was black, and her right arm was in a cast from elbow to fingertips. Steeling every emotion I had, I barely acknowledged Jordan and Robbie sitting in chairs next to her bed and willed myself not to cry as I rushed over to her.

She opened her "good" eye and looked at me before a tear leaked out and streamed down her swollen cheek. "I don't like you seeing me like this."

I noticed she was missing a tooth from the right side of her mouth as she spoke. I wanted nothing more than to find my father and beat him with a tire iron.

"Where is he?" I asked through gritted teeth, vibrating in rage I could barely contain.

"In jail where he belongs," Robbie said tiredly, staring at me with pain in his brown eyes.

I looked at our mother, then to my brothers. "For how long?"

"At least the weekend. The deputy told us there's a bail hearing Monday," Robbie replied.

The poor kids were only fifteen and seventeen and should not have to shoulder this burden. I pulled twenty bucks out of my wallet and handed it to the eldest, Robbie. "Go home, order a pizza. I'll stay here."

"We don't want to leave," he argued, trying to give me back the money.

I shoved it back at him. "Just go, I'll be there in a little bit."

"Please, boys," my mom said weakly. "There's a lasagna in the freezer too. I was going to cook it tonight, but…"

"Shh," I told Mom. "It's okay, they won't starve." I stared at my brothers, who looked defeated and exhausted. A glance at the wall clock showed past 12 a.m. "Go home, get some rest, and I'll call you if anything changes."

They reluctantly left after each one kissed Mom on the cheek.

Still trying to hold my emotions inside, I pulled up a chair close to her bed and grabbed her hand that didn't have the cast on it, stroking my thumb across the top. "Tell me what happened."

She glanced at me with her good eye and shook her head as another tear leaked out. She craned her face toward the window, where a bright three-quarter moon shone surrounded by stars. "It doesn't matter."

"It matters to me," I said with a sigh.

"Please, baby. Please, I don't want to talk about it."

I lifted her hand and kissed it. "Were the boys there when it happened?"

She sniffed, another tear leaking. "Yes, Robbie tried to stop him. He says he's okay, but I saw him holding his ribs where Harlan punched him."

I hated that I was named after my father. I hated it so much. And my younger brother was obviously following in my footsteps, trying to defend our mom against this monster. I was proud of the kid, but like me, it was a burden he shouldn't have to bear.

"I'm going to the pack with this," I told her. "This cycle of abuse ends tonight."

She turned her head to face me once again, alarm coloring her eyes. "No, baby, please don't." She always called me *baby*. Deep down I knew she couldn't bear to call me by my name because it reminded her of the prick she was married to.

"It won't end unless they intervene. The only other option is... I kill him. I'll gladly go to prison. It'll be worth it."

Just then, the door opened, and a nurse entered. "Hey there. Visiting hours are over, unfortunately, and I need to get her vitals. Do you mind?"

I shook my head and let go of Mom's hand as I stood. "Of course not. Could you please give her something to help her sleep?"

The older nurse had kind eyes and looked at me with sympathy. "Of course. I planned on it anyway. She's due for her pain meds."

"Thank you," I said to her. Then I looked at Mom. "I'll be back in the morning." I kissed her forehead. "I love you."

"Love you, baby," she said weakly as the nurse injected a needle into her IV line, and I watched Mom's eyes fluttered shut.

I raced down the hallway to the stairwell and sprinted down the four flights, fighting emotion until I got to my bike.

Once I put my helmet on and started the engine, I broke down and I fucking cried. "I'm going to kill you, you fucking bastard," I growled absently to my father who was probably sleeping soundly in a jail cell. I started the bike and headed toward my house to check on my brothers.

7

THE THIRD HUNTER

After Face had sent over all the information in an email to Psycho, et al, signed by Viper and the Nighthawks, we'd received a phone call immediately, inviting us to their clubhouse for a meeting.

Once we arrived, I held back a laugh at the setup of the clubhouse. It was not too dissimilar to ours, with apartments, a breakroom, offices, and even cages or cells to hold people. Or, perhaps wolves. Guessed he wasn't joking when he said they policed their own.

Psycho stood in the center of the warehouse as Viper and us five lieutenants stood around in our cuts, boots, and jeans.

"Thanks for coming," Psycho said, flanked by Demon, as before. "We were very impressed at the information you sent us."

Viper nodded. "You're welcome. I'm sorry we don't have an ID on the third hunter, but hopefully that was enough to get you started on capturing those two."

Face had run a full background on Leland, the other brother, and found out he worked in the Quarter as a bartender, but he only worked during the day for the day-drunk crowd which explained why he wasn't home when we had raided the house. Lyle worked in the offices of the Mercedes Benz Superdome doing some kind of computer job.

"Yes, but we'd still like help IDing the third hunter. Do you have anything at all?" Psycho asked us.

"No, but if we could speak with the witness, that would help," I said.

Psycho looked at me, hesitated, and then said, "No, I don't think that would be wise."

I lifted my chin. "Why not?"

He glanced at my vampire brothers and replied, "She doesn't trust vamps."

I chuckled. "That's why I'm volunteering for tribute."

He and Demon had a quiet conversation between them, and then he looked at Viper. He pointed at me. "She only talks to him."

"Agreed," Viper replied, knowing we'd already discussed this.

"Is she here now?" I asked, looking around.

Psycho rubbed his fingers over his long-ass beard. He narrowed blue eyes at me. "Yes. You stay, the rest of you can go."

"Phoenix and I will be outside," Viper whispered in my ear, too low for them to hear.

I nodded and waited for my brothers to clear out. Demon led me to an office off to the side of the clubhouse and told me to sit in one of the chairs in front of the desk. He offered me a beer and some food, but I declined.

After leaving me alone in there, I looked around and saw photos of Psycho with a woman I presumed was his old lady. There were a few photos of children I also assumed were his. The rest of the office was unremarkable; just a desk, a computer, and a wall calendar. I grinned at the three big red circles on it during the full moon cycle.

The door opened and Psycho walked in with a shy-looking young woman. She was fairly thin and there was uncertainty in her blue eyes.

"Venom, this is Kalissa," Psycho said, introducing us. He instructed her to sit in the office chair set behind the desk.

She looked at Psycho. "Who's this? A cop?"

He shook his head. "No, just someone from another club.

They're helping us find the hunters who hurt Donny and Pax."

She bounced her gaze between me and Psycho. Then, she said to me, "You're a wolf as well."

I could tell she was one-hundred percent human and wondered how she figured it out.

I nodded. "That's correct. I won't hurt you, I promise."

Psycho stood in the corner of the office with his arms folded across his cut. "I'll be here the whole time, honey."

She nodded.

I watched her posture and wondered what had happened to this girl. She sat with her shoulders hunched forward and her hands in her lap. I could tell it was painful for her to make eye contact. I had to tread lightly here.

I set my cell phone on the desk and pointed to it, asking Psycho, "Is it okay if I record? My memory's shot in my old age." I smirked.

He nodded and I turned to Kalissa as I hit record on the app like Face had shown me. "Can you tell me what happened?" I asked her. "Just start at the beginning."

She glanced at Psycho, who nodded in encouragement. Then, she looked at me and cleared her throat. "Me and Donny and Paxton parked down at the wharf and were heading toward the place where we could buy tickets to go on a dinner cruise. It was me 'n Donny's six-month anniversary. Paxton met a lady on one of those dating apps, and he was meeting her there as well for a date."

"Go on," I urged.

She nodded slightly. "We kinda had to park far away, you know, it was a Saturday night 'n all. When we passed some bushes, these three guys jumped out at us. One of them grabbed me around the back and put his hand over my mouth. The other two jumped Donny and Pax and shoved needles into their necks. They made me watch while… while…" Her eyes filled with tears and her voice hitched. "They took big knives from their belts and cut out their hearts while they were sleeping from whatever drug they'd given them." Psycho offered her a box of tissues and she took one. "I tried to scream, kick, and get away, but the guy was just too strong."

I reached over and put my hand on hers. "Then what happened?"

"The guy holding me pulled my head back by my hair, but he still had his hand around my mouth. He said…" Her voice hitched again, and a tear leaked down her cheek. "He said, 'See what happens when you go around fucking wolves? We did you a favor, lady. They would have killed you eventually. Stay away from werewolves, especially that motorcycle gang. It'll end in nothing but pain and death for you. If not from them, then us. Do you understand?' I was staring down at Donny's body in disbelief, but could hardly see because of my tears. Then he said, 'Bitch, tell me you understand!' and I nodded my head just to get him to let me go."

She looked at Psycho, then me, dabbing at her eyes with the tissue. "Then he punched me in the head so hard I passed out. When I woke up, I was lying on top of Donny's legs in that bush. I screamed and screamed and screamed until some people walking by heard me and called nine-one-one. The ambulance took me to the hospital where I called Psycho after they examined me. I hate hospitals and just wanted to go home, so I told them he was my brother so they would let me leave with him. I don't care what those guys said, I wasn't going to stay away from Donny's 'family', even if just out of spite for them killing him. The more time that goes by, the angrier I get."

My blood was boiling. These hunters had to be stopped. Just the fact they'd assaulted a woman like that had me shaking with barely controlled fury. I kept my cool, though. I took a deep breath and asked her, "So then you spotted them again later, I'm told?"

She glanced at Psycho, and he again nodded. She looked down at her hands. "Yes, I was coming out of my clinic downtown to meet my mom for lunch and saw those guys eating at the café across the street. It has these big floor-to-ceiling windows and I recognized them right away. Unfortunately, I never got a good look at the guy who'd held me while those other two monsters killed Donny and Paxton. I pulled out my phone and hid behind a big stone column in front of a building, snapping as many photos as I could. I was shaking so bad I'm sure the pictures were blurry, though."

"I saw the photos, they weren't bad," I said, smiling at her. "Our tech guy was able to clean them up some. Is there anything you remember about his voice? The way he smelled?"

She looked down, deep in thought. "He didn't talk like he was from Nawlins, or even have an accent at all. And he wore Eternity for Men cologne, and I only know that because my ex-boyfriend…well, not Donny, my other ex… he wore that, and I hate the smell of it now 'cause of him."

"Stupid question, but this guy wasn't *that* ex, right? The one who held you and put his hand over your mouth?"

Kalissa laughed, but it was devoid of humor. "No. My ex was no taller than me and way scrawny. This guy was big and beefy. Like you guys." She pointed to the both of us.

I said, "I'm six-two, and I'd say Psycho here's about six-five. Stand up."

She did as she was told. "I'm gonna come behind you and give you a bear hug, okay?"

"Okay."

I slowly put my arms around her and held her loosely with both my arms locked around her chest, her arms down by her side. "Was he about my height?"

"Yes, his head was above mine. But not as high as Psycho's would be." She looked over at him.

I didn't want to let her go. She smelled like strawberries and vanilla, and I felt relief by wrapping her in my arms so protectively. But, I did let her go. I was fond of my head and figured Psycho would take it off if I didn't stop touching her soon.

"This is super helpful," I said, going back to sit in my chair. Then I looked at Psycho. "I find it a little odd they didn't wear ski masks or something. Don't you?"

He nodded. "I do. But something tells me they aren't too bright."

I looked at Kalissa. "Or they just don't give a fuck."

"That too," he replied. "Stupid and brave will definitely get you killed."

"I agree. We're going to catch them, Kalissa. We already have a lead on two of them."

She nodded. "I know. He showed me their photos, the mugshots, and the driver's license pictures. That's definitely them... the ones who killed..."

I put my hand on hers. "I know. We'll get this third guy, okay?"

"Thank you," she said, her eyes filling with tears once more.

I stopped recording and put the phone in my pocket. "We'll be in touch." I fist-bumped Psycho and showed myself out of the clubhouse.

Phoenix and Shadow were waiting for me in the parking lot, sitting on their bikes talking.

"How'd it go?" they asked me when I mounted my Harley and started the engine.

"Pretty well," I said over the loud rumble. "That poor girl is pretty traumatized though. I wanna find this third fucker and shove my fist down his throat and then tear his head off."

Phoenix's eyebrow shot up. "Wow, okay. Let's get back to the clubhouse and see what you got."

I took off out of the lot, leading the way back to the Nighthawks' hangout.

8

REGRET

Kalissa

I sat on the toilet lid in my small bathroom and frowned at all the wrappers I could see scattered on the bed in my room. Empty packages of cream-filled pastries, donuts, candy bars, bags of chips, and crackers… and I had been doing so good. I sighed.

After flushing away my shame, I wiped my mouth and scrubbed the smell of vomit and chocolate out of my mouth with my toothbrush. I went into my room, swiped all the wrappers to the floor, and lay on my bed, arms and legs sprawled out. I stared at the ceiling fan as it spun around slowly.

Donny had helped me get better. He had told me that I didn't need to be thin to be attractive. He told me he preferred women with some "meat on their bones" and that there was nothing shameful about food. He constantly cooked for me, and while he was a good cook, he didn't know that I would just go throw it back up in the small bathroom of his mobile home where I used to spend so many nights with him.

But after a while, I did stop with the bingeing and was able to keep food down. And yes, I'd put on a few pounds, but my counselor, Alice, had told me how to handle it. To not panic or see the scale rising as a bad thing—that it was a positive thing. She had helped me decide on a goal weight and once I reached it, we were going to come up with a new plan on how to maintain that weight without starving myself or purging after a meal.

I hadn't seen Alice in months since Donny died. She'd called to check on me, but I had avoided her calls. What was I going to say? Sorry, my boyfriend was a werewolf and some hunters cut his heart out in front of me? No, I was sure she'd slap about ten more psych diagnoses on me, and that was the last thing I needed. So, since Donny had passed away, I'd had a few bad binges but mostly, I was tapering off them. I knew the physical toll it took on my body to keep shredding my stomach with all the vomiting. I had admittedly cut way down on what I ate just so I could avoid throwing up, but today... I couldn't take it.

After talking to that Venom guy and having to relive the whole thing, I'd driven straight to the grocery store, loaded up on junk, and of course came home and binged on it. But, like every time before, while the delicious snacks helped to spike that happy spot in my brain, it was temporary. The self-loathing and sick feelings quickly came over me, and I once again found myself face-first in front of the porcelain god as my fingers found their way down my throat to make it all come back up. All the while, regret and shame washing over me in waves.

I really should call Alice. I know she's worried about me.

Glancing outside my window, I saw the car parked there and breathed a sigh of relief. The Bayou Wolves had me under protection, and because I refused to live in their "clubhouse" as they liked to call it, I insisted on being in my own home. Besides, I had to keep up some kind of normalcy with my family. They had met Donny, and they knew he died, having believed he'd been stabbed in a robbery gone bad. And they most certainly hadn't known he was a werewolf. Hell, there were some days where I couldn't wrap my brain around it still to this day.

I remember meeting Donny in that coffee shop, as I couldn't stop staring at him or his "club brothers"—humongous guys in leather vests. I wanted nothing to do with a motorcycle gang, but my little naïve self couldn't stop staring. I'd grown up very simply in an average neighborhood and went to average schools before getting a job as a nursing assistant in a small walk-in clinic downtown.

"Like what you see?" Donny had asked me with a chuckle.

I was sure I'd turned fifteen shades of red. I'd quickly looked straight ahead, wishing a hole would appear in the floor and swallow me up. After getting my coffee, I'd left the shop and hurried to my car, but Donny and his friends were on their motorcycles talking. He'd approached me and explained he wasn't in a gang and had asked me out. I wasn't sure why I said yes, except that I was attracted to him and told myself to live a little. I had nothing exciting in my life.

My cat, Mr. Sparky, jumped onto the bed and curled up next to me. I petted his head and instantly felt more relaxed with him beside me.

Donny hated Mr. Sparky and the feeling was mutual. I knew why now, but when they first met, I couldn't understand it.

I again closed my eyes, remembering the day I'd found out Donny was a wolf.

"I have to go away for a few nights."

I turned around from the fridge where I was looking for a cucumber to cut up for a snack. "Why? Where are you going?"

He looked nervous, and I hadn't seen that look on his face before.

"Just tell me," I urged, pulling the cucumber out and washing it off.

"Just a club thing, baby," he said, coming to kiss me on the lips, but he seemed hesitant and on edge.

I should have accepted that, except he had said the exact same thing last month, and the month before. Three nights with his club buddies and no mention of where they were going or what they were doing. It made me suspicious.

Instead of asking more questions, I shrugged. "Okay, have fun." I began cutting up the cucumber.

He wrapped his arms around me from behind and said, "I love you. I'll see you in three days."

I said nothing as he walked out of my small house, got on his bike, and rumbled away.

After seasoning the cucumbers, I sat on my sofa and pulled up the app that would tell me where Donny was as I ate. I felt like such a psycho chick for doing this, but without any explanation, I had to know where he went. I was proud of myself for not having gone through his entire phone while he was in the shower yesterday morning. I'd just installed the app, hid it, then put the phone back on the nightstand. I didn't feel in my gut that he was cheating. It was something else, something more sinister.

After a couple of hours, I checked the app again to see he was somewhere near the Mississippi, but far away from the Quarter. I'd lived here my whole life and couldn't picture in my mind exactly where he was. It had to be remote.

"Well, Mr. Sparky, looks like I'm going on a little trip," I said to the cat, getting up and going into my room to throw on a pair of sweats and a hoodie. I grabbed my keys, purse, and phone and hopped into my little Jetta. The app had a map that helped guide me to the location. It only took about ten minutes to reach the water's edge and I soon found myself surrounded by a bunch of old abandoned buildings and warehouses with busted-out windows and shrubs of overgrowth all around them.

I turned the car off and quietly exited, using the phone to guide me closer to Donny's exact location. I froze when I heard a very frightening howl pierce the quiet night. I looked up at the very full, fat moon against the clear, star-shot sky above me and sniggered at the ridiculous thoughts of werewolves that ran through my head.

"You read too many books," I grumbled to myself and kept walking.

What I saw next knocked me on my ass. Donny and a bunch of his "club" friends were writhing around on the ground, tearing at their clothing. One large white wolf was pacing back and forth as if it was supervising. Every once in a while, it would rear its huge head back and howl at the moon.

What. The. Fuck!

I practically shoved my whole fist into my mouth to keep from screaming when I watched Donny, now buck-naked and shiny with perspiration, get on all fours and begin to stretch and transform. Dark hair sprouted from every inch of his body and his face elongated into a large snout. A tail sprouted from his backside, and as I looked on in horror, where Donny once stood was now a big brown wolf, shaking itself like a dog.

I couldn't breathe. My head began to spin and my vision swam in and out of focus. I dropped the phone and then landed with a thud on the ground, where the darkness took me.

Shuddering at the memory, Mr. Sparky's licks and meows bolted me back to the present. The wolves had found me passed out and could only drag me with their teeth into a nearby warehouse until the next day when they had their human bodies back and could drive me home.

Donny had a lot of splainin' to do.

God, I missed him.

I thought back to the conversation today with that Venom guy and wondered what his story was. He seemed very chill, sweet even. He had kind brown eyes and I could tell he was a little older by the salt-and-pepper in his hair and beard. He spoke calmly and I couldn't imagine him transforming into a wolf like Donny and Psycho did.

He also smelled really, really good. When he had his arms around me during his "demonstration" I wished I could have told him to just stay like that a few more minutes. It made me feel safe, and he was so warm. His arms and chest felt hard with muscle, but protective as well.

I shook my head at my stupid thoughts, knowing I needed some time to deal with Donny's death and not start thinking about other men.

"But it's been months, Kalissa. Maybe you need to move on," said the angel on my right shoulder.

"Nope, you need to grieve some more. Misery makes you stronger," said the devil on my left.

"What do you think, Mr. Sparky?" I asked the cat, knowing he wouldn't answer me.

He just nudged his head into my side, then fell asleep purring. I wasn't far behind him.

9

SINS OF THE FATHER

Boulder, CO – 2001

My cousin Jeramy punched the wood paneling of the wall closest to him and swore. "He did fucking *what*?"

"He's in jail until Monday but I don't have plans to let him make it home after he's let out. I certainly ain't posting his bail."

Aaron, his younger brother, looked at Jeramy and said, "We better call Dad," then picked up the phone and start dialing.

Their dad and mine were brothers. How one was a wife-beating bastard and the other was the poster boy for a good, ol' American family man, I didn't know.

Aaron set the phone back on its cradle on the wall. "Dad'll be here in a few."

Jeramy and Aaron were around my age and shared a small house that they rented together.

I paced the floor, chewing my thumbnail. My body was tired from lack of sleep, but my emotions and brain had me bouncing around like a crackhead.

"What are you gonna do?" Aaron asked, fear and curiosity in his big brown eyes.

"I'm gonna kill him, that's what," I gritted out, the picture of my mom's face flashing in my mind again. "He's always been an abusive bastard. Grabbing her too hard, shoving her around, sometimes a slap or punch, a whipping, or calling her names, but never something like this. She wouldn't tell me what happened."

"Sounds like a pretty bad fight," Aaron said.

"Were the boys there?" Jeramy asked, referring to my brothers.

I stopped pacing and looked at him as he leaned against the wall. His arms were folded across his chest as he stared at me. "Yes. Robbie tried to stop him, but Dad punched him in the gut. I need to check on him, Mom says she thinks he might have some bruised ribs." I raked my hand through my hair. "Fuck!"

I pulled out my flip phone and saw three missed calls from Amanda and one from Robbie. I let Amanda know I was fine, and then dialed Rob's number.

He picked up on the first ring. "Harlan. Where are you?"

"I'm at Jeramy's. Are you all right? Mom said Dad punched you in the stomach."

"Yeah, I'm fine, just sore. I'll live."

"And Jordan?" I asked.

"He's good. Sent him to stay at his buddy Seth's for a few days. His mom will take them to school on Monday."

"Okay. Tell me what happened."

I heard him blow out a breath.

Just then, my uncle walked through the door. I looked at him, then the phone. "Robbie, I'm gonna put you on speaker. Uncle Will is here."

"Hi, Uncle Will," he said softly.

"Hey, boy. You all right?" Will asked.

"Yeah, I'm good. Anyway, Mom was making dinner and Dad came home from work in a really shitty mood. I mean, shittier than normal. He asked Mom what was for dinner, she said she was gonna heat up that lasagna from the freezer she made the other day. They got into an argument about him having to eat 'leftovers' even though it wasn't. I heard her say earlier in the day she was tired and had a headache and didn't want to cook. It just escalated from there, man. Mom stood up for herself, and when I heard them arguing, me 'n Jordan rushed into the kitchen to see Dad grab the closest thing to him—the mop. He started hitting her with it. I tried to grab it from him, and he punched me so hard in the stomach I fuckin' puked. Jordan rushed him, but Dad just pushed him down. He hit Mom with the mop handle over and over… broke her arm as she was trying to defend herself. Fucking asshole."

I shuddered at the visual. I'd heard enough. "Okay, bro. Go hang out with some friends."

"No, I wanna be here when Dad gets home," he said, sounding braver than I knew he felt. "I'm gonna kick his ass."

"Well, then you're wasting your time because that motherfucker is never coming home. I'll be in touch." I ended the call and looked up at my uncle, whose face was stormy with rage.

"How long has this been going on? The abuse?" Uncle Will asked me, his jaw bunching.

I glanced at my cousins, then looked down. "Our whole lives."

"You can't be serious," he snapped, his brow furrowing.

"It goes back as far as I can remember, just never *this* bad. It's like he's getting worse," I said, blowing out a breath.

"And here I was, proud that none of us had turned out like our bastard of a father," he murmured, pinching the bridge of his nose.

I never knew my grandfather—he'd died before I was born. My grandmother, either. I was told they died in an accident. Then, it clicked. I pointed at my uncle. "You guys killed him, didn't you?"

My cousins gasped. He looked at them both and reluctantly nodded. "Yes, after he killed our mother. She wasn't a wolf like yours is though. Too fragile as a human, couldn't heal from the wounds."

I knew once the next full moon came and my mom shifted, all her injuries would heal. But that was neither here nor there as far as I was concerned. She still had to suffer in pain for another three weeks, and even three minutes was too long as far as I was concerned.

I looked up at my uncle and said, "I need the green light from the pack to take him out."

My uncle immediately shook his head. "No, we're not repeating history. I won't allow it."

Slamming my fist against the nearest object—the top of the TV—I said, "It already has repeated itself! We should just let him live? Next time, he'll fucking kill her, Will, and you know it!"

"I'm with Harlan on this one," Jeramy said, looking at his dad.

Uncle Will shook his head again. "No, we go to the police."

I scoffed. "And what, send a wolf to prison? Oh yeah, that'll go over well. After he slaughters the other prisoners and half the guards on the first full moon... I'm sure they'll be able to keep him there."

"Dammit!" Will said, sliding his fingers through his salt-and-pepper hair.

"Death is the only option!" I snapped.

"I vote yes," Aaron blurted.

"I vote yes, as well," Jeramy said.

"You're the pack leader but you're outnumbered, Uncle," I said, lifting my chin.

He made a laughing sound, but he wasn't smiling. "Well, Harlan's in the pack too. I'm sure he'll vote no."

"Fuck him, he doesn't get a vote," I snapped.

"I doubt Becky's gonna vote yes," he replied, looking at me.

Rebecca was their sister. She had no kids and lived like a hippie. And he was right, she'd never condone violence.

"Regardless, it's still three against two since my dad doesn't get a vote. The minute he's released from jail, he's getting a bullet to the skull. I'll make it fast."

Will lifted an eyebrow. "You have a gun?"

I grinned but I felt no happiness, just pure, unadulterated vengeance. "No, but ol' Harlan's got plenty and I know where he keeps them."

I sat in the car, my knee bouncing with nerves. I looked at my cousins, Jeramy in the front and Aaron in the back. "I told you guys I could handle this. I don't need you staining your souls with this shit."

"Fuck Uncle Harlan, I want to see him dead too," Jeramy said with a scowl, zipping down the window and spitting a stream of tobacco out. A bad habit he'd recently picked up. "He's always been an ass to us, too."

"Same," Aaron said from the backseat.

Uncle Will had relented and had agreed to go to my dad's bail hearing and then report back to us. The hearing started fifteen minutes ago, and I was about to explode with nerves.

"What the fuck is taking so long?" I murmured, resisting the urge to chew off every last fingernail.

Jeramy snorted. "Right? What's the crime rate in Boulder? It can't be that high with all the yuppies and hippies living here."

Finally. My cell phone rang. I flipped it open. "Hello?"

"It was 500 dollars bail. I just posted it. He should walk in about thirty minutes when they get all the paperwork straightened out. They also issued a restraining order on behalf of your mom," my uncle said.

"Thanks. We're outside the courthouse now."

"Be careful. Gotta go." He hung up.

I rolled my eyes. Whatever. One shot to the head, how dangerous could it be?

As I waited for Dad to walk out, I thought back to earlier today when I'd gone and visited Mom.

She'd looked better now that a couple of days had gone by. The magic in her blood had sped up her healing process, but she was still bruised in some areas. The swelling on her eye had gone down and she could open both easily enough and was sitting up, talking, and was able to feed herself and use the remote control for the television to keep her occupied. It had made me happy to see her getting better, but the rage inside me had not quelled one bit. I was on a mission to kill my father and would rather apologize to her than ask for permission.

No… ya know what? I wouldn't apologize at all. Killing him would be doing my mom a favor. I hoped he had life insurance to take care of the house and the bills, but if he didn't, whatever. I'd work two jobs to take care of her. The woman hadn't worked outside the home a day in her life, and I knew she had nothing.

"How's Robbie? Is he okay? No broken ribs?" she asked, stroking my face with her good hand.

I kissed her on the forehead. "Nope, just sore. I'm sure he's healed up by now." I winked at her, as the nurse was in the room changing out her IV.

"I'm glad. I've been worried about him." She sighed. "He's just like you. I know you tried to help me before… and I appreciate it." She looked down in shame.

"Mom, you need to leave him. Before he kills you." I stared into her sad, tired eyes.

She shook her head and rubbed her hand over her cast. "I know, but I don't have any money or anywhere to go, baby. Besides, if I just play nice and not make him angry, everything will be fine. He's not a monster, you know. He has his sweet moments. He's just, you know, under a lot of stress at work, and needs to learn a healthy outlet for it."

My eyebrows shot up. "And you think letting him slap you around… or in this case, almost kill you, is a 'healthy outlet'?" I asked, putting up air quotes.

"No, no, not at all. I'm just saying, like therapy or maybe going to the gym or something to expel his energy." She forced a smile at me and patted my hand. "It'll be okay. I'll make him his favorite meal and dessert to appease him. I'm sure he'll be quite angry from having to be in jail all weekend, but I can handle it."

I couldn't believe what I was hearing. She was all ready to take him back. Resume life as normal.

"Mother... you don't need his abusive ass! I have a good job now. I'll get a second one and we'll help with the bills. Robbie's already looking for a job too. We will be fine without him," I urged her, desperation lacing my every word. Even though I already knew I was probably going to kill him.

"No, no, baby. That's not a burden you need to bear. You go live your life with your nice girlfriend. How is she doing, by the way?"

There was no getting through to her. Yep, Harlan Lahey, Sr., was gonna die.

10

WOLF LESSONS

Venom

After I'd played the recording for Viper, Phoenix, Shadow, Kovah, and Face, they looked around the table at each other.

"So, we basically have nothing," Kovah said, lifting the beer bottle to his lips.

"No, we don't have nothing, mister glass-is-half-empty," I said, glaring at the hybrid.

"I agree," Face said. "White guy. Six-foot-two-ish, wears a specific cologne, not from around here, associates with the Manchester brothers. I think we can find this asshole."

Throwing Kovah a smug look, I said, "See? Face is on it."

"Face is always on it," Face replied, chuckling.

"I don't know what the fuck we'd do without you," Viper said.

With his gaze down, looking at the tablet, he replied, "Eh, Jemini's catching on pretty quick." He looked up at us. "But, I'm glad I'm not just another pretty face."

"Now, who would ever accuse you of that?" I asked, biting back a smile.

He laughed. "Oh, I don't know. Just, like, everyone my entire life."

I didn't smile at that. Yeah, the guy was ridiculously good-looking. Chiseled face, trim, muscular body, even a spray tan (I wondered when he'd give those up and just embrace the pale like the rest of them), but I never stopped to wonder how people treated him. I knew how people with disfigurements, overweight people, overly tall or overly short people, and others who weren't deemed "average" or "normal" were treated, but what about those who were exceptional?

"Are you fucking listening at all, bro?"

I looked up to see Phoenix talking to me, the other lieutenants staring at me in expectation. I cleared my throat. "Sorry, what was the question?"

Viper sighed. "Are you going to talk to this Kalissa chick again?"

I furrowed my brow. "The hell if I know. Why would I need to?"

All four vamps and one hybrid all chuckled at once.

"What's so damn funny?" I asked.

I was met with silence. Just their knowing grins.

Leaning back in my seat, I pulled a toothpick from the inner pocket of my jacket and stuck it in my mouth. "You fucking vampires are weird as hell."

"We heard your heartbeat speed up when we mentioned Kalissa's name," Phoenix admitted with a grin.

Assholes. "So, you set me up?"

"Eh, yeah, pretty much," Kovah replied with a snort, setting his beer bottle down.

"I'm worried about the poor girl, that's all," I defended. "You didn't see her. She's thin as a rail and her eyes were just... haunted. She's scared out of her mind. And traumatized as fuck."

"I believe it," Viper said. "But one's heart doesn't speed up out of care and concern. Only feelings of love and infatuation."

"You like her," MyAnna, his wife, teased.

"I agree," Bloome said with a wink.

I glanced at her then back to Viper. "It's just concern. Now stop this middle school shit."

They were pissing me off. I had no feelings for this girl. I just felt sorry for her. I couldn't imagine watching someone I loved get their heart cut out.

"Whatever you say," Shadow teased.

I ignored him. "Yeah, whatever. The answer is no. No need to talk to her again."

As if on cue, my phone pinged with a text: *I think I remembered some more. Can we meet?*

The number was unknown, but I didn't need to guess who it was. Psycho must have given her my info.

With all my club brothers staring at me, I replied: *Sure, Kalissa. I'll pick you up from the BW clubhouse in thirty.*

She replied thanking me and then I looked up at the group, who were all staring at me.

"Your heart is beating in, like, double time," Gabe said, not even trying to hide his grin.

"Oh, fuck off. All of you." I got up from the table and added, "I'll be out late. Don't wait up."

They were still sniggering.

I stopped, then I looked at Bloome. "Hey, why do vampires not want to become investment bankers?"

She looked up from her phone and lifted an eyebrow.

"Because they hate stakeholders!" I mock-stabbed Shadow in the chest with an invisible stake.

They all groaned. The girls giggled.

I walked out of there whistling casually. Couldn't let them know how lowkey excited I was to see Kalissa again.

"Do we have Psycho's blessing to be meeting alone?" I asked, realizing how weird that sounded.

Kalissa hopped on the back of my bike and wrapped her arms around my waist. It felt good... right... to have her on the back of my bike.

"Yes, he said it was fine," she replied, yelling over the sound of the engine and the helmet I made her wear.

I sped off out of the lot and headed downtown. I knew this small restaurant that was near the Quarter but wasn't very well known. Still public enough but quaint and not crazy busy with tourist traffic.

I parked the bike at the entrance and helped her off as she removed the helmet. I strapped it on the back of the bike and prayed nobody would take it. Not that it had ever happened before, but I trusted no one. As I held the small diner's front door open, she walked through. We were seated quickly and handed menus.

I set mine down and looked at Kalissa. "Talk to me."

She also set her menu down and pierced me with sad blue eyes. "I remembered something else about the night Donny was killed."

"I'm sorry that you've had to relive this over and over. We just want to catch these guys so they don't hurt more wolves," I said.

"Or vampires?" she replied.

That came out of left field. "What do you mean?"

"That's what I'd remembered after I talked to you. The guy said that after he killed Paxton. Right before I was knocked out. 'The bloodsuckers are next.' What does that mean?"

I drew in a breath and steeled my emotions so I didn't give too much away.

"Coffee?"

We both looked up to see the server wearing a classic diner uniform of a yellow dress and an apron, smiling down at us holding a steaming coffee pot.

"Sure, I'll have some," I replied, turning my cup over.

Kalissa waved her hand and shook her head.

"What do *you* think it means?" I asked her once the waitress had walked off.

She ran her finger along the edge of the plastic menu and then glanced up at me. "I've heard the wolves talk about vampires. I thought they were teasing. You know, like *Twilight* jokes."

I furrowed my brow until I realized what she meant. "No, they weren't joking. What did you hear?"

She ignored my question. "So… vampires exist as well?"

I nodded slowly. "Yes. The Nighthawks. They're vamps."

Kalissa chewed her lip, and I found the little wrinkle that formed between her brow endearing. "So, you're a wolf but your club is full of vampires? How does that even work?"

With the steaming mug paused at my lips, I said, "It's a long story I'll tell you about one day. Just not today."

She nodded and stared at the menu. "Can I get some food?"

I turned my head, curious. "Of course. Why wouldn't you?"

She shrugged and I found this odd.

"Order whatever you want." I looked down to see they had burgers and that was good enough for me.

"What have the Bayou Wolves said about vampires?" I asked.

She shrugged. "Nothing really. Just to beware of them and all that."

Huh, interesting, considering they'd asked for the Nighthawks' help.

"And Donny, did he ever speak of vampires?" I asked.

She set the menu down. "No. Never. He hated the fact that I

knew he was a wolf."

"That brings me to my next question, how did you find out he was one?"

"What can I get you?"

I looked up at the server and ordered a double bacon cheeseburger and Kalissa ordered a soup and sandwich combo.

"Comin' right up. Y'all want Cokes too?"

We both nodded before she walked off.

"So?" I asked, anxious to hear this story.

Kalissa chewed her lip again and looked at me, this time something close to guilt or shame coloring her features. "I... followed him one night."

My eyebrows hit my hairline. "Well, I'm sure that was quite an unpleasant surprise."

"You have no idea," she replied, looking embarrassed.

She went on to explain everything, watching them shift and turn into wolves, and then finished by shaking her head. "I should have just trusted him. Trusted them."

I shrugged. "I can't say I blame you. I mean, giving no explanation at all seems shady. I would have probably done the same thing." And I meant it. That dope couldn't have made something up? Anything?

"You would have?" she asked, surprised.

I chuckled at her reaction and said, "Yes. I mean, I'm pretty sure."

She darted her gaze around the small diner before asking me, "How long have you been a wolf?"

Her question confused me. Did that Donny cat tell her nothing? "Well, my whole life, darlin'. I was born this way."

She sat back in her seat, her movements making the shiny red material squeak under her movements. "Huh. So, unlike the movies, you can't be bitten or like, scratched and become one?"

I shook my head. "Nope, total myth. By birth only. Keeps the bloodlines pure."

"And you have to mate with another wolf to have kids?" she asked.

The wonder and curiosity in those big baby blues made me smile without my permission. She was so damn cute I couldn't help it. I stared intently into her eyes. "No, we can breed with humans."

Her eyes went wide temporarily and then she tried to hide it. "So, then you just have human kids?"

"Nope," I said with a popping sound. "Pure wolves. We don't have our first shift until about age eighteen, so it's not like the woman would give birth to a puppy, because I can tell by the way those wheels in your mind are spinning that that's what you're thinking." I ended on a chuckle at her wide-eyed reaction.

"Well, ya got me there. I was thinking that." Her lips twitched.

I leaned back in the booth and grabbed a toothpick from the holder on the table before popping it into my mouth. "But you don't have to worry about that anymore because you're not with a wolf. I'm sure you'll go on and find you a nice human guy. If you were smart, you would."

11

MONSTER LESSONS

Kalissa

I could not shovel the grilled cheese sandwich into my mouth fast enough once the sever set our food down. How was I going to tell this ridiculously handsome, charming, and tough guy that I was most likely ruined for all human men for the rest of my life after being with a big, strong, protective wolf?

One, who apparently, had kept lots and lots of information from me. *Damn you, Donny.*

I watched as Venom chuckled at me as I ate. He swabbed his French fries in ketchup and didn't break eye contact with me as he slowly inserted them into his mouth and chewed.

I had never wanted to be a French fry so bad in my life.

Suddenly, I had a strong desire to lick the ketchup off his beard. God, that beard was so sexy. Donny didn't have one, and at this moment, I suddenly realized that I really, really liked beards.

A question popped into my mind, and I was so glad for the distraction. After I took a sip of my soda, I said, "So, surely your real name isn't Venom?"

He grinned at me. "What was Donny's club name?"

I pursed my lips together. "Dawg."

Laughing, he said, "How apropos."

"What does that mean?" I asked, lifting the spoon to my lips and blowing on the tomato soup. The bread from the half sandwich was probably a million carbs, and that one big bite I took was all I planned on eating. I really had just wanted to order a salad, but I knew how guys got when they took girls on dates and they only ordered a salad.

"This isn't a date, you moron!" The angel on my right shoulder was correct. This wasn't a date. Why did I care what this guy thought about my eating habits?

"Because you have issues, Kalissa," the left shoulder devil replied.

"Harlan," he said.

I blinked at him over the steaming bowl. "Excuse me?"

He grinned, the burger at his lips. "That's my name. Harlan. Lahey. Nice to meet you."

"Oh," I replied, probably turning as red as the soup I was about to slurp off the spoon. "Sorry. Kalissa Morgan."

"Kalissa's a pretty name. Any meaning behind it?" he asked.

I got this question a lot and didn't like it because I didn't have a very exciting answer for it. "I'm afraid not. At two days old, I was left on the doorstep of a fire station and the note said that was my name. My parents kept it." I shrugged. "It's pretty, I like it."

"I agree. It suits you. You ever find your birth parents?" he asked, wiping his mouth with a napkin. He had crumbs from the bun in his beard and I wanted to lean forward and brush them off for him.

Shaking my head, I said, "Nah, never did. My adoptive parents are pretty amazing. My birthmother must have had a reason to need to give me up. If she comes looking for me, I'll answer the call. But… I'm content where I am." And it was the truth.

"I'm sure she did, too," he agreed. "We have some great resources and a tech dude who's a whiz at finding people if you ever wanna track her down. Door's always open." He smiled sincerely at me, and it made my stomach do a little flip-flop.

How could I be crushing on this guy so soon after Donny's death? It wasn't right. I should grieve some more, just like the little devil keeps telling me to.

Clearing my throat, I said, "So what about you? Family?"

He went on to tell me about his family back in Colorado and how his parents had passed away. He didn't say how, and I didn't ask. His brothers still lived there. "So you moved here for the motorcycle club? The Nighthawks?" I asked.

He shook his head. "Not exactly."

His curt answer made me think he didn't want to talk about it, so I didn't pry. Maybe I would see him again and I could get answers then.

Why do I even care! He's a damn wolf, I don't need to go through this again. He's not even human!

Deciding my inner musings were right, and my women's intuition was kicking in, I said, "Hey, after we eat, can you take me home? I'm pretty tired." It was a lie. I wasn't tired. I'd rather invite him into my house and see what his lips and beard tasted like, but I had to stay away from men like him. Wolves like him. He seemed sweet and genuine, but I knew, like all wolves and motorcycle club members, he must be harboring a seriously dark side.

Harlan walked me up to the door of my little house. I looked over his shoulder to see one of the Bayou Wolves sitting in a car out front and frowned. He appeared to be asleep.

He followed my gaze and his brow furrowed. "Who's that?"

"Club guy. They got round-the-clock surveillance on me."

"Looks like pretty tight security they got there," Harlan replied dryly. "Maybe I should stay on your couch until the guy wakes up from his nap."

Or you could just sleep in my bed with me.

Stop it, Kalissa!

I smiled. "No, it's okay. I'll text Psycho and he'll call and wake him up. That's Gordy, and he likes his naps."

Harlan lifted an eyebrow. "Well, Gordy needs to get himself some energy drinks or something to stay awake, because that is not cool." He jutted his thumb behind him at the car and seemed genuinely pissed off.

I bit my lip. "I know."

"No need to text Psycho, I'll wake him on my way out. Unless you'd like me to stay on your couch for the night. I'm a little leery of their security, especially since those hunters are still out there."

He was right, but for some reason, I didn't think I was their priority. They seemed too excited to hunt werewolves and vampires. "They would have killed me already if they wanted me dead," I said with a shrug.

"I understand that," he replied, his hands in his pockets as if he was trying to keep from touching me. "But they warned you to stay away from wolves, and here you are, surrounded by them."

That was true, I hadn't thought about that. "I guess."

"I think you should come to the Nighthawks' clubhouse with me. We have a spare apartment equipped for humans. You'll be a thousand percent safer there than here. I could be killing you right now on your front step and ol' Gordy over there would probably be snoring right through it."

I looked at him in horror. "A vampire's lair? No, thank you! I think I'm safer here in my own house." I began to dig through my purse for my keys, thinking about all the vampire books I'd read.

Harlan grabbed my arm and spun me around to face him.

I looked down, still digging through my purse. *Where are the damn keys?*

He used his finger to force my chin up to look at him. "Do you actually think I would take you somewhere that you'd be in danger? More than this?" He waved his hand at the car where

Gordy now had his mouth open and was fogging up the windows with his breaths.

I chewed my lip again and shook my head. "No, but vampires terrify me, Harlan. How do you feel so at ease around them?"

"I think you've been watching too many movies. They're just people. Think of them as having a non-contagious virus where they need blood instead of food, and a sunlight allergy. They don't turn into scary-looking monsters when they feed, and they don't attack people. Viper's very specific about them feeding from willing donors only."

I gasped. "People volunteer to get bitten?"

He chuckled, and the sound sent another round of butterflies into my stomach. It didn't go unnoticed that he was still touching me, his warm hand now on my cheek instead of my chin. "Yes, it apparently induces, uh… erotic feelings. Or so I'm told."

Just like the feelings you're inducing in me right now… I cleared my throat. "Well, I don't think Psycho will allow that."

Harlan grinned. "Are you a member or prospect of the Bayou Wolves?"

I shook my head, my brow furrowed. "Of course not."

"Then it's settled. Let's go." He turned around and took several photos of sleeping Gordy with his phone and began to climb the steps down toward the street. But I just stood there, unsure what to do. Was I safer with him? Were those hunters going to come after me and kill me for associating with wolves since they'd told me not to? Did they know that Harlan was a wolf? What if I went with the Nighthawks and the hunters found out they were vampires and they still killed me for associating with them, too?

"This isn't up for debate," he said, grabbing my hand and dragging me down the stairs.

I stomped my foot and dug my heels in so he couldn't pull me. "Hey! I'm trying to make a decision here. I need a minute. Please."

He stared hard at me, and then I watched as his features softened. His kind brown eyes seemed to be filled with something close to regret as he came toward me. "I'm sorry. Let's go inside for a few minutes. You got any beer?"

I immediately relaxed and nodded my head. "Donny left a six-pack in the fridge. I don't drink, so it's all yours."

We went inside, with Gordy still snoring his head off in the car, and I set my purse down on the counter. Mr. Sparky meowed and ran toward me, then stopped short when he saw Harlan. Immediately, his hackles went up and he hissed at the werewolf. Harlan chuckled. "Cats don't like us."

"I know," I murmured. "He hated Donny, too." I watched as Mr. Sparky backed away from Harlan and ran back into my room.

"Beer's in here?" he asked, laughing at the cat's antics as he pointed to the fridge.

I nodded. "Yep, help yourself."

He opened the fridge and frowned, grabbed a bottle, then twisted off the top. After closing the door, he said, "You don't have much in there. Do you need me to take you to the store?"

Shit. I plastered on a smile. "No, just haven't had time to go. Been busy at work. Eating out and such."

It wasn't a complete lie. I did only eat about once a day so why stock a fridge if the food was just gonna go bad? It was easier to grab a salad or a protein bowl on my lunch break.

"Where do you work?" he asked, twisting off the top and tossing it in the trash can.

"I'm a nursing assistant for a small walk-in clinic downtown."

He took a swig of the beer. "That sounds interesting. Do you like that?"

"Yes," I replied truthfully. It was a fun job and I had good bosses and great benefits. "Which brings me to my issue. If I stayed with you at the Nighthawks' place, would I still be able to go to work?"

Harlan set the bottle on the counter and folded his arms across his chest. "How much vacation time do you have saved up?"

12

DAD MUST DIE

Boulder, Colorado – 2001

I pointed my finger at my cousins. "Stay in the car."

"No," Jeramy said, opening the door.

"I mean it," I snapped. "In fact, take the car, go home. You can bring it back to me later. I should have just dropped you two off." I blew out a breath. I wasn't thinking straight. I had a one-track mind, a plan: beat Dad home, grab a gun, lie in wait, shoot him as soon as he walked through the door.

"We want to help," Aaron said from the backseat.

"You'll be in the way. Look, just stay here. When your dad pulls up with mine, duck down so he don't see you."

"Fine," Jeramy said. "But if I hear anything going on in there, I'm coming in."

"Me, too," Aaron said.

"You'll hear a gunshot or two. Wait a few minutes after that, if you must." I got out and slammed the door, leaving them in the car, hoping they'd listen to me. I used my key to unlock the front door to the house and ran inside to my dad's gun safe in their bedroom. Once I'd turned sixteen, Dad had given me the combination in case I ever needed a gun to defend the home in the event of a break-in.

Guessed he was going to regret that decision here very soon.

I opened the heavy door and saw two rifles and an assortment of handguns, along with boxes of ammunition. I decided the shotgun would make too much noise and only held five rounds. I wasn't a bad shot, but I had to make sure this fucker died. I picked up a 9mm pistol and loaded a magazine with sixteen rounds. I shoved it into the well and charged the weapon before stalking out to the living room to wait for him.

Thoughts of, *Are you seriously going through with this?* and *You're going to actually kill your own father?* were racing through my mind. I put them aside. The only way to protect my family was for him to cease to exist because I was sure the next time, he would kill her. I knew trying to talk him into just leaving wasn't going to work. He was too damn stubborn and proud.

With all the lights off, I sat in the semi-darkness of the room. It was still daytime, but I had all the shutters and curtains closed. I was glad my brothers were at school. They didn't need to see this. After a few agonizing minutes, I heard a car pull up, and then a car door slam.

My father's heavy footsteps slowly slogged up the walk to the porch. With my sensitive hearing, I heard my uncle tell his sons to get in his car. They didn't argue, and I was sure it was because my father would hear them. I heard the car pull away and drive down the street. Good, I was glad they were gone. In case the police got involved, at least they would be nowhere around.

Keys jiggled and the knob turned. My stomach flopped with nerves, and my palms were sweaty. I wiped them on my jeans.

Dad immediately spotted me sitting in his recliner. He pulled the blinds open and said, "What the hell are you doing sitting in the dark?"

I had decided a few minutes ago that I would give him one chance, and one chance only to agree to get out and leave us alone. It was the only way I would be able to live with myself, to say, *at least I gave him a chance*.

I lifted the gun and said, "Pack your shit and get the fuck out. I'm helping Mom file for divorce, and you will give her everything, including the house."

He eyed the gun and had the nerve to smirk at me. "I don't think so. Everything your mother has is because of me. I've busted my ass for over twenty years to pay off this house and keep the lights on. Put clothes on all of your backs, make sure you had food in your bellies. And you have the goddamn nerve to come up in here and threaten me with *my* fucking gun, making demands?"

His arrogant reaction wasn't surprising, but the fact he had so much bravado caught me off guard. I would have shit myself if someone pointed a loaded gun at me. "You almost killed her, you asshole. You need to leave."

He set a brown paper sack down on the front table and shook his head. "Stop being such a drama queen, she's fine."

"She has a broken arm, two bruised ribs, an eye that's swollen shut, and you knocked out one of her teeth. She most certainly is not *fine*. Not to mention the fucking emotional trauma. How she's put up with your ass all these years, I will never understand."

"Because she knows her place. She knows she has nothing without me. She'll be much more obedient after this, anyway. You'll see once you find a wife."

"I will *never* be like you," I seethed, narrowing my eyes at him.

He snorted, putting his hands on his hips. "You'll see. Bitches need to be put in their place."

I shook my head. "So, jail was worth it? You're lucky it wasn't a full moon, you idiot."

"Watch your tone, boy." He pointed a finger at me.

I sat forward in the chair, still aiming the gun at him. "Pack your shit, and get out. I'm not going to ask again."

He folded his arms across his chest and raised his chin. "So, what? I don't leave and you shoot me?"

"That's the plan. Last chance."

"You ain't got the balls, junior. Now, get out of my house. I need a shower."

Without getting up, I raised the gun and fired a shot. His eyes widened and he moved out of the way at the last second, diving to the ground as the round embedded itself into the wall behind him.

I stood up and stalked toward him to fire another round at close range into his head, but as soon as I got close enough, he grabbed my legs and I was slammed down onto my belly, the gun falling from my hand and clattering to the floor. Dad spun me over and jumped on top of my torso. He threw punches at my face and head while I tried to buck him off. I looked over and could see the gun to my left. While trying to avoid getting punched, I clawed the floor for the weapon, but it was just out of my reach.

"Get off me, you dick!" I screamed, trying to block blows while punching him in the side and back.

"I'm gonna kill you, you little prick!" he hollered, that raging hate on his face I'd seen so many times. Then, he wrapped his hands around my neck and pressed both thumbs to my windpipe, squeezing—hard. I reached up and tried to peel his fingers from my neck, but they were so tight. I was running out of oxygen while he smiled down at me. "You're dead, little man. *Dead.* I'm gonna bury you in the backyard like a fuckin' dog."

"Help," I wheezed, not sure who I was talking to but knowing I was going to die. I tried reaching up to poke his eye or scratch his face, but his arms were too bulky and in my way. Once the room began to swim and out of focus, and things started to go black, I barely registered the sound and light of the front door opening.

I heard a bloodcurdling scream and realized it was my mother. "No! Get off him! He's just a kid! Please, Harlan. Please stop! No!"

"Oh, my God!" said another female voice.

"Help me," I wheezed.

I saw my mom's face looking down at me as she jumped on Dad's back and began smacking him in the head with her cast. "Get off my baby!" she screamed.

That loosened his grip a little for me to get in a couple of huge breaths. He backhanded her off, where she went flying to the floor. When he heard me cough, he began to squeeze my throat once more.

Looking to my left to see if I could reach the gun, I watched in horror as it was picked up. An ear-splitting pop was followed by chunks of blood, bone, and brain matter raining down on my face and head seconds before my father's body slumped down on top of me, a huge, bloody hole in his forehead with his eyes still wide open. I pushed him off and rolled over, staring at the ceiling and grabbing my throat while I coughed and breathed in much-needed oxygen.

I looked over to see my mom on her knees on the floor, the smoking gun in the lap of her dress with her good hand still around its grip, staring blankly at my father's body.

"I've called nine-one-one, Sarah," Aunt Becky said, wrapping her arms around Mom's shoulders. "You'll be okay."

My uncle and cousins rushed inside and gasped.

"What the hell happened?" Uncle Will asked, his eyes wide.

"Holy shit," Jeramy breathed.

"We were parked around the block, heard the shots," Aaron said.

I sat up and crawled over to my mom. "Mama, are you all right?"

She slowly moved her gaze from my dad's body to me. "Baby… why… why did Harlan have a gun? Was he going to shoot you?" Her eyes filled with tears, and she rubbed at my neck, which I was sure was probably very red. "You need an ice pack…"

I glanced at Will, who cleared his throat and looked at me wide-eyed. "You guys got into an argument, he went into his room, and grabbed the gun from his safe, didn't he?"

Slowly nodding, I looked at Mom and Aunt Becky. "Um, yeah. I, uh, told him to leave, to divorce you. He laughed at me and went and got his gun, told me to get out. We wrestled for the gun, and he dropped it. But then he started to choke me, and… and…"

"I think we get the gist, son." Uncle Will helped me stand and put me and Mom on the sofa.

Sirens screamed outside, and I knew the story Will had just helped me concoct was the one I'd have to stick to. Premeditated or not, my father was dead.

13

RUNAWAY THOUGHT TRAIN

Venom

We walked into the clubhouse slowly, my way of trying to make Kalissa feel welcomed and not intimidated. After she informed me she had two weeks of vacation saved up, I told her that should be plenty of time for us to dispose of these hunter assholes, and then she should be able to get back to her life. She packed a bag, arranged for a friend to feed her cat, and we left the house, with ol' Gordy still sleeping in his car. I'd texted Face everything, including the photos of him, and told him to let Viper know that I was bringing the girl back there.

Everyone was waiting in the main part of our warehouse-turned-clubhouse when I brought her in through the front door.

She stared with wide blue eyes and adjusted her bag on her shoulder. "Wow, y'all are so… so… big. Like the wolves."

A few chuckles echoed. I introduced her to everyone and let them know she'd be under my personal protection. She visibly relaxed when Jemini, Bloome, and MyAnna took her to the breakroom and showed her around. Kalissa looked back at me briefly and I nodded and smiled, as if to let her know it was okay to go with them.

"Face showed me your messages," Viper said, coming to stand next to me once Kalissa was out of earshot. "I called Psycho and let him know what was happening. He wasn't too happy about us essentially taking her from them, but after he saw the photos of his guy sleeping on the job, he didn't have much of an argument. I let him know I was informing him out of courtesy and wasn't really asking for permission."

I nodded. "Very good."

"How is she?" he asked.

"She didn't seem too concerned about the hunters until I broke it down for her. About how her continuing to consort with wolves could get her killed. She was under the mindset that they would have killed her that night if they wanted her dead. She didn't realize she was left alive to send a message." I shook my head.

"To be so naïve and carefree," Viper said with a sigh.

"Right?" I agreed. "She's taking two weeks of vacation time from her job, effective immediately, so I think we need to wrap this thing up so she can get on with her life."

Viper looked at me, biting back a smile. "Face ran a full background on her."

I looked over at him and raised an eyebrow.

"Well, ya know, just protocol for anyone who's going to be staying here. And just FYI, she's totally clean. Zero issues or criminal record."

Furrowing my brow, I said, "So what? I don't care."

He chuckled. "Just thought you'd want to know, that's all."

Turning to face him fully, I said, "Vane, I'm not getting involved with this girl. Humans are trouble." Realizing what I'd said, I quickly added, "I mean, I'm glad it worked out for you, but I've been there. I'm older than you, I've had a few experiences."

"You're not older than me. I was born in 1956. And you...?"

I sighed. "1983."

"Ah, the Eighties. Great decade. Saw Journey three times in concert that year."

"Point taken," I murmured. The guy was, like, maybe thirty when he was turned. I was pushing forty. It took a lot of brain power to wrap my head around their immortality. I wasn't envious of it, though. No thanks. "Well, I'm hungry."

"I'm shocked," he replied, laughing as he walked away.

I popped my head into the breakroom and looked at Bloome and Kalissa with my phone in my hand. "What do you want on your pizza?"

"Everything," Bloome said. "And those cheesy breadsticks. Oh! And a Pepsi."

Shadow smacked her on the butt. "Mmm, yeah, put some more jiggle on this ass."

She elbowed him and bit back a smile. "My ass is big enough, thank you very much."

I looked at Kalissa expectantly.

She shook her head. "I'm okay. I ate earlier at the restaurant, remember?"

"Yes, I do. You ate one bite of a grilled cheese sandwich and three spoonfuls of tomato soup. And two sips of pop." I looked at my watch: 12:15 a.m. "That was six hours ago."

She looked stressed, and this confused me. "Pizza's on me, darlin'. I got coupons," I said, trying to make her feel better. Was she worried about money? How could she not be hungry?

"No, it's fine. I only eat like once a day, so I'm good."

"Well, it's Sunday now, so you ate yesterday. Time to eat again," I urged, tapping my watch.

Jemini grabbed my arm and led me out of the breakroom. "Let me help you place that order, old man."

Once we were out, she looked up at me. "Don't force her to eat. I think she may have some kind of issue with food."

I furrowed my brow. "How do you know that? You just met her."

"First off, I have killer intuition, made even better after I was turned. Two, look at how thin she is. Three, she said she only eats once a day. Also, I got this cousin… same look on her face when food was mentioned or pressured on her. We found out later she had some kind of disorder."

"Shit," I said, raking my hand through my hair. "I'll go apologize."

She grabbed my arm. "No. Don't do that, it'll make her more self-conscious. Just let her deal with it. Leave food out of the conversation if you get my drift."

"But I love food," I whined.

She laughed. "Yes, we all know. Now, go place that order before Bloome finishes all of the Hot Pockets out of the freezer."

"Nooo! Not the Hot Pockets!" I joked, sliding my finger over the phone and pulling up the pizza place's app.

After I placed the order, I went back into the breakroom. Jemini and MyAnna were sipping on blood mugs. MyAnna's read, *Fuck this, I'm moving to Transylvania* with a picture of a castle. Bloome sat drumming her fingers on the tabletop.

"So you two drink blood but you can eat food?" Kalissa asked Bloome.

"I'm a witch, not a vamp. Blood, gross." She made a face.

"Pizza, gross," MyAnna said over the rim of her mug.

I stared into her big brown eyes and said, "You haven't been turned long enough to hate pizza. I mean, that's got to be the last thing to go once you start hating real food."

She giggled. "You're not wrong."

"I miss pizza." Jemini sighed.

Kalissa looked at Bloome. "You're a witch? Seriously? Like Wiccan and all that?"

She lifted a shoulder. "Eh, sort of. Wiccans are, like, a less serious branch of witchcraft, that's the only way to explain it. My parents are witches; therefore, I'm one, too."

I could see Kalissa wanted to ask her more questions but decided not to.

She turned to the others. "So, how long have you two been, ah, vampires?"

"Less than a year, both of us," Jemini answered.

"Is it awesome?" Kalissa asked, her chin resting on her hand.

They prattled on about being vampires, which I tuned out, and just stared at the blonde-haired beauty listening to them with rapt attention. The sleek planes of her cheekbones and jaw. The blush on her cheeks. Her eyes the color of sapphires. The way her hair shined under the fluorescent lights. Her slender shoulders, the swell of her breasts under the button-up shirt she wore. The way her jeans fit over the curve of her slim hips.

Stop, Harlan. Stop.

I scrubbed a hand down my face and turned to leave the breakroom but was met with a wall of a chest. Along with a deep, rumbling chuckle.

"You need to just sack up and ask her out on a date."

I looked at Phoenix. "Just keep an eye on her for a few minutes, all right?" I asked, pushing past him and toward the back door. The pizza order wouldn't be ready for another thirty minutes, but surely I could find something to do that didn't involve walking around here with a damn boner.

After a short drive, I parked in the lot of the pizza place and sat on my bike while I thought about what I was going to do with Kalissa. At this point, it was just stupid to deny my attraction to her, and I'd been around long enough to know she was attracted to me, too. Just the way her body instinctively leaned into mine when she was around. The way she didn't fight my hand on her face outside of her house earlier. The captivating attention she gave me when I spoke. But her boyfriend had just been murdered a few months prior and I needed to have some respect. Give her some space. Besides, I told myself I wouldn't get involved with a human ever again.

And why was that, exactly?

Let me count the reasons. One, they didn't know about wolves and it would freak them out. Well, guessed that excuse wouldn't fly with Kalissa, now, would it? Two, I was getting up in age. Most human women I met were older and had already had kids or were in the midst of a divorce or some kind of ugly mess I wanted no part of. Kalissa had told me she was thirty-three. She could still have kids, I supposed. How does a human woman even deal with their offspring being full-blooded werewolves? I couldn't do that to someone. Three, humans were fragile. They broke and died easily. At least female wolves were tough. My mom… she was weak emotionally, but she recovered quickly from all the injuries my father had inflicted on her over the years. Kalissa was weak and human, especially with how thin she was. Did Jemini really think she had some kind of eating disorder? Maybe she was wrong. Some people were just naturally thin.

I realized my excuses, aside from the fact she was still grieving, were pretty flimsy. I also decided I was suffering from hunger and needed food in order to stop this silly runaway train of thoughts in my head, so I made the decision to wait inside the joint for my food.

I killed the engine to the bike and put the kickstand down. I hadn't taken one step when I heard and felt someone breathing too close behind me. I whirled around a split second before I felt the stab of a needle in my neck. I recognized Lyle Manchester and punched him in the nose before I fell to the ground and blacked out.

14

CURIOSITY
Kalissa

I glanced at the wall clock and saw it read after one a.m. Admittedly, I was pretty hungry. I had told Venom—Harlan—that I didn't want pizza, but I had decided to let myself have one slice to keep him from looking at me the way he had earlier. I didn't like that. It was the way my father had looked at me when I was little. How, if I ate too many snacks, he would glare at me as if I had just committed some kind of biblical sin. I'd told Harlan earlier that I was happy with my adoptive parents, and I was, for the most part, but my dad was pretty controlling. He was also extremely frugal and limited what we ate, how much my mom could spend on groceries, what time the heat or A/C was allowed to be on, and everything else you could think of that cost money.

By the time I was about twelve years old, I'd been conditioned to eat everything on my plate in order for it to not go to waste. I quickly caught on that if I dished my own food, I could just take smaller portions. That way, not only were there leftovers for him to take to work the next day that would make him happy, I wouldn't have to eat until I was sick just to "finish my plate."

"Something's wrong," Bloome said, setting down her phone. "He's not answering, and the pizza place is only like five or ten minutes from here. He should have been back by now."

"What's the problem?" a big red-haired guy with a name patch reading *Phoenix* asked as he came into the breakroom.

Bloome looked at him and I briefly wondered if they were related. They looked like they could be brother and sister.

"Harlan's not back with our food and he's not answering his phone."

"Viper, Shadow, Face, get down here," Phoenix yelled after he'd walked out of the breakroom.

"Maybe the place was just busy?" I suggested, trying not to panic. I knew nobody here. I only agreed to come if I could stay close to Harlan. Why did he even leave? Why couldn't someone else go pick up the order? How do you transport pizza on a motorcycle anyway?

Jemini put her hand on my arm, and I immediately relaxed. "Shh. It's okay, sweetie. The guys will handle it."

A guy who looked just like her but in boy form popped his head in. "What's going on?"

"Venom's not back from his pizza run," she answered.

The guy glanced at me then at her. "So?"

"It's been close to an hour," Bloome supplied.

"Kalissa, this is my twin brother Jermaine," Jemini said.

"Hi," I said. "You guys are definitely twins."

Then, they stared at each other without saying anything. It went on so long I started to get uncomfortable. I got up to leave, but she put a hand on my arm again. "It's okay. We'll find him."

Jermaine left the breakroom, and I folded my hands on the tabletop. "Twin telepathy?"

Jemini smiled. "Smart and pretty. I like you."

"I read about it in a book," I deadpanned.

"Oh, you like to read?" she asked, and I knew she was distracting me.

A guy named Face—and I could see why—popped his head into the breakroom, holding up an iPad. "I got a lock on his location. You look after her." He looked at the ladies, pointing at me.

"On it," the three women answered.

"Oh, and if you want to watch," he said, setting the electronic tablet on the table and pulling out a smartphone. "I'm trying out new video software. I expect feedback."

I was confused. "What, like that high-pitched squealing sound? I don't think that will—"

He chuckled. "No, like a review. If it's good software or not."

I felt my cheeks heat. "Oh, okay."

He rushed out and I heard the front door open and close, and their motorcycles start up.

Bloome took something out of the microwave and put it on a plate, then handed it to me. "Hot Pockets. I think that one is cheese and ham. You know, since the pizza's a bust."

I stared down at the food and cleared my throat. "Thanks."

"Sorry, it's all we have. Me, Venom, and Kovah are the only ones who eat food here, and I spend half my time at my actual house, so food's sparse."

"Who's Kovah?" I asked.

"He's another lieutenant. He's with his wife right now. She's some federal cop and he's always with her."

I nodded, not really caring. After pulling the sandwich apart to let it cool, I took a cautious bite. *Oh, my God, that's good.*

After a couple of bites, I started to feel guilty. I shouldn't be eating this. I stared down at the food in disgust.

MyAnna rubbed my back. "Don't worry, I'm sure the guys will find Harlan."

"Huh?" I asked, looking up from the plate of self-loathing. Oh. They must have thought I was worried about Venom. And I was… but being late picking up pizza wasn't some earth-shattering emergency. These guys were all huge and tough. I was sure they'd find he'd just run another errand or something.

"I hope those hunters didn't get him," Jemini said, using the small case the tablet was in to prop it upright so we could all watch. Right now, the screen just showed a blue and white logo of some kind. No video.

Hunters! Oh, shit. What if they got him? It would be all my fault. I suddenly felt sick, like I wanted to throw up. "Um, is there a bathroom here?"

MyAnna went to a small corkboard on the wall I'd just noticed and plucked a key from a hook with the number 200 above it. She handed it to me. "That's the guest suite. It's accommodatable for humans. There's a toilet, sink, shower, and bed in there. It's all yours."

"Um, thanks. I just need the, uh, toilet for now."

She walked me to the door of the breakroom and pointed to a stairwell that led to a bunch of closed doors with numbers on them. Sort of like a motel or apartment hallway, but it was open.

I tried not to run up the stairs. I unlocked the door, shoved the key in my pocket, and quickly found the bathroom. I could barely get the lid up before I was heaving what I'd just eaten into it.

After I was finished, I felt better, but my stomach was still a bundle of nerves. *Please, God. Let him be okay.* I flushed the toilet and found some small paper cups in a drawer. I used one to rinse out my mouth with water. A further search revealed a bottle of mouthwash and I swished with that before looking at myself in the mirror. I had dark circles under my eyes and honestly, I looked like hell. The little amount of makeup I'd put on earlier was sort of smeared under my eyes and the blush and highlighter were long gone. I just looked pale and gaunt. I thought about how Alice had told me I needed to gain some weight healthily, and I knew she was right, but right now, I just needed to get through these two weeks in this den of vampires and hope everyone made it out alive.

That's the guest suite. It's accommodatable for humans. MyAnna's words echoed through my mind. Humans? Did vampires not use the toilet or shower? Or sleep? I thought about all the books I'd read. Sometimes they did and sometimes they didn't when it came to fiction.

Well, they had to need a bed. Where else would they have sex?

Because I know those girls downstairs were having lots of it, I could tell by the way they looked at their guys. I wondered if Harlan brought women back to his suite, and then I wondered which one was his.

God, I have got to get out of my own damn head. This was a temporary situation, and after these two weeks were over, I was outta here. Back to my job, my house, my cat.

I laughed at my own ridiculousness and took the stairs back down to the breakroom, where the three women and Jermaine had their gazes glued to the electronic tablet. I stood behind them and watched.

"We found his phone," Phoenix said, holding it up for the camera.

It appeared someone was filming him, probably that Face guy. I would bet he was the resident nerd here. A very fine, sculpted nerd at that, but too pretty for my taste. *To each his own.*

He put the cell phone close to the camera, and I could see it looked beat-up. The screen was cracked, and the blue and orange Denver Broncos case was scratched and torn at the edge when Face flipped it over for the camera. Then he panned in on a motorcycle I was sure was Harlan's and my heart sank. "That's his bike, all right. Phoenix, you drive it back." Sounded like Viper's voice and I heard keys jangling. Did they all keep keys to each other's motorcycles?

"Fuck, that's not good," Jermaine said. I just now noticed he was sipping on a coffee mug that read *Witches Do It Magically* and a broom underneath it.

"I agree," MyAnna said.

"Harlan's a tough fucker. He wouldn't go down without a fight. I bet someone took him, then left his phone there so we couldn't track him," Jermaine said.

I felt sick again. "Why would someone take him?" I asked.

"That's what they're going to find out," Jemini said, placing her hand on my forearm again. When I looked into her pretty green eyes, I immediately felt calm once again. Was she using some kind of vampire hoodoo on me?

I watched as the men huddled up in the parking lot. Shadow joined the circle and said, "The employee says the pizza order was never picked up nor did Harlan come in. I showed him a photo."

"Fuck," Viper said, raking his fingers through his hair.

"Wait, is that blood?" Shadow asked, pointing. The camera followed his movements as he bent down and touched something on the ground next to the motorcycle. After dabbing his fingers in it, he put it to his nose. "Human."

"Collect as much as you can," the person operating the camera said.

"Face got DNA collection and analyzing going on in that office of his as well?" Jermaine asked his sister.

She shrugged. "I haven't seen anything along those lines. Can't hurt to have the blood, though. Maybe he's got a hookup at the local crime lab?"

So, it was Face filming.

"Oh, probably. Knowing him," MyAnna answered, staring at the screen. "I'll ask Vane later."

"Who's Vane?" I asked.

"Viper," they replied in unison.

"Oh," I replied, my cheeks heating. "Sorry. Just trying to learn everyone's names."

Bloome smiled at me. "I know, it's hard to get used to. I think they should just all use their real names unless they're out in public. I never call Craig 'Shadow', ever."

"I think Harlan's a cool name. How'd he get to be called Venom, anyway?"

They all looked at each other questioningly.

"Uh, actually, I don't know?" Bloome replied. "I thought it was a snake thing but maybe not. I'll ask Craig."

"It's okay. I'll ask him myself. Then I'll spill the tea later." I winked at them.

"Nice," Jermaine said, fist-bumping me.

The tablet showed the blue logo on it again, so I figured they were probably trying to work out a plan or something.

"I have a question," I said, sliding my hair to the side and braiding it.

"What's that?" Jemini asked.

"How come y'all don't have… uh, what are they called? Club whores in here? The Bayou Wolves had them. Big-boobed slutty women everywhere!"

Bloome wrinkled her little freckled nose. "Hell no. They aren't needed around here. The single boys go get blood whores and hook up with them. No trash like that allowed up in here. I'd be beating ass every day if one touched my man."

I laughed. "Well, most of the wolves are single, so that makes sense."

"What's a club whore?" Jemini asked.

I had read a lot of "MC" books in my obsession with reading romance, so I answered, "I think they're there for the, uh, needs of the club members. But I noticed this place doesn't have a nightclub like the wolves do so I guess it would be pretty awkward to just have slutty women walking around here."

"That's where you're wrong, girlfriend." MyAnna stood and grabbed my hand. "We do have a club. In fact, I should go check on it. Vane puts me in charge of the Cobalt Room when he's gone. Let's go."

15

BROTHERS GRIM

Denver, Colorado – 2006

Amanda and I had been together five years, and I felt it was time to propose. She, of course, had accepted and talked nonstop about wedding plans. Honestly, it was starting to grate on my nerves a little, but of course, I knew better than to say anything.

She was still working in the front office of the warehouse, and I was still in the back slinging car parts. Amanda had been with me through my mother's criminal trial. A particularly nasty district attorney hadn't believed Mom's story about self-defense and felt she had shot and killed my father out of vengeance for her recent beating, making a production out of the fact he had been shot from behind. Thankfully, there was a compassionate jury, who took pity on her thanks to the very expensive attorney my Uncle Will, Aunt Becky, and I had hired, who allowed Harlan's priors to be admitted as evidence. I had photos of all her bruises and black eyes, as well. After my testimony on the stand, and the pictures of my neck and face where he'd beat me black and blue and tried to kill me, they acquitted her in mere minutes. It had taken me three years to pay back my uncle, who'd dipped into his retirement funds for the money, for my quarter of the attorney fees, but I'd done it—with lots of overtime and hard work.

However, the stress it had put on my mom had caused a serious decline in her health. Every full moon she'd shifted, and it had healed her painful joints and weak bones, but it hadn't been able to heal her mind. She was riddled with guilt over killing her husband

and continued to maintain that she should have just "hit him with a frying pan" instead and let him live. She was sure he'd be so very sorry and apologetic about trying to murder his son and putting her in the hospital.

There was no getting through to her. It made me sad, but I'd given up years ago trying to get her to see things for the way they were. All I could do was pay for a therapist and hope she got through to my mom. Thankfully, Dad had a pretty good life insurance policy through his union at work and Mom paid off the house and his car, and had enough left over to pay monthly bills. Sadly, she stopped taking care of herself and had to be admitted to a care facility, where she pretty much refused to eat and had to be manually fed through a tube. She didn't want to live, and I couldn't help but feel responsible for that. She was in her late fifties and had a lot of life left, but I supposed she felt like she didn't deserve it, nor want to live it without Harlan. I couldn't wrap my brain around it at all, and it pained me to see her in such a horrid condition, literally wasting away at her own doing. Every month, my brothers and I had to check her out of the facility for three days so she could shift. Even as a wolf, she refused to hunt, instead just lying in the grass and sleeping all night. It was horrible and devastating to watch.

I woke up from sleeping all day and looked at the clock: 4:22 p.m. I stretched before slogging out of bed to the bathroom. I brushed my teeth and used the toilet, then went out to the kitchen, where Amanda was cooking.

Apparently, she was in quite the mood because she immediately launched into a tirade, picking a fight with me about my working hours, and then she threw the sauce-covered wooden spoon at me in anger. When I tried to console her, it made things worse. She accused me of working the graveyard shift to avoid spending time with her, to get out of wedding planning... and everything else she could think of.

Deciding she was PMSing or something, I went back to the room and closed the door. The full moon was tonight, and I was already on edge and had zero patience for her fits. I had given my boss some bullshit religious excuse about needing to pray in the direction of the rising sun and setting moon for three days a month, which got me out of work while I shifted.

Being it was summer, I had a few hours until the moon came up, but decided to leave early, anyway. My brothers and I were going to get some burgers and beers before our shift. I kept a duffel of clean clothes, soap, and a toothbrush and paste in my car to clean up once morning came after the shift so I could go home and sleep as if I'd been at work all night. It was an exhausting ruse to keep up and I constantly wondered how long I planned to do it before I told Amanda the truth. How was I to keep this lie for the next fifty years? Not to mention, once she got pregnant, she'd need to know that her children would be wolves. I was ashamed I'd let it go on this long.

I kissed her cheek and she scowled at me. "It's only five thirty. You don't have to be at work 'til eleven. Where are you going?"

"Gotta meet my brothers to discuss Mom's care plan," I said. Not really a lie, but not the whole truth either. We always discussed Mom when we met for dinner.

"Whatever," she said, waving me off. "I'll just eat another meal alone. Again."

I kissed her cheek once more. "I love you." I went to the front door, got in my Mustang, and left.

"Ya gotta leave her, bro," Robbie said to me before taking a bite of his burger.

I set down my beer and narrowed my eyes at him. "You should talk."

"What?" he asked around a mouthful of food.

"Your chick's a fuckin' psycho wolf," Jordan said, shaking his head at Robbie.

"Hey, cool it," I told Jordan. "I don't think that's necessary."

"Well, she is. How many times have you had to replace a car window or tire?" he asked.

Robbie took a swig of beer and said, "Well, I did cheat on her, so I kinda had it coming."

"Most chicks just talk about going all Carrie Underwood on their man's car. They don't actually do it," Jordan commented, chuckling.

"She apologized," Rob defended.

"Yeah, after you threatened to take her wedding budget away," I replied.

Robbie set his beer down and put his hand on top of it. "But seriously, when are you going to tell Amanda? You can't keep going on like this."

"I know," I replied, feeling guilty. "I think I should probably just make up some BS excuse and break up with her."

"Or just cheat on her and let her find out," Robbie said with a smirk.

I shook my head. "First, no, I don't get down like that. Two, I like my Mustang just the way it is. Unbroken windows and tires without knife holes in them."

Jordan took a sip of his chocolate milkshake and set it down. "So, you don't want to be with Amanda then? Because the way I see it, if you thought she was the one, your soulmate and all that crap, you'd show your wolf to her and pray she accepted it."

He was right, and it was a thought I'd had many times over the last few years. Amanda and I got along fine, for the most part, but this whole nagging me about the work schedule thing and the wedding had gotten worse over the past few months. I was beginning to see a different side to her. Sure, nobody was perfect, including me, but I wasn't sure how much I could put up with for the rest of my life. I also was about ninety percent sure she would flip the fuck out and not want anything to do with me after she found out my secret.

I dipped a fry in some ketchup and said, "You guys are right. I need to stop this before it goes any further. We've already put deposits on two things for the wedding and I need to pump the brakes. I just know she'd never accept that side of me." I looked around the retro fifties diner and lowered my voice. "I'm fairly sure she'd lose her shit if she saw my wolf."

"So, what are you gonna do?" Robbie asked.

"Break up with her, I guess." I sighed, the thought making me sick. I glanced at my watch. "We need to get Mom and head to the mountains."

After paying the bill, I drove to Mom's care facility to pick her up for our "monthly outpatient visitation." I left my brothers in the car to wait, and after signing the book, I went to turn toward the hallway that would lead me to her room. Suddenly, loud siren noises erupted, and someone announced over the loudspeaker, "Code Blue room 215."

That's Mom's room!

I sprinted down the hallway and saw nurses doing chest compressions on her still form. She was on her back, her eyes closed. Her frail body jerked with the movements of the compressions. Someone pushed me out of the way, dragging a medical crash cart.

"No!" I yelled, running toward her. "Mama!"

A large, older guy in scrubs pulled me back by my arms and told me to wait outside. I stood in the doorway as they used electronic paddles on her for several minutes.

I flipped my phone open and hit a button. "Get in here now!" I barked down the phone to Robbie and then hung up while I watched in horror as they worked on Mom.

My brothers arrived within seconds, skidding to a halt and then watching with tears in their eyes as they pronounced her time of death.

"No," Jordan said, now openly sobbing. "Mommy. No."

I was trying to keep my shit together for my brothers. They

were only twenty-one and nineteen. Adults but still kids.

"I'm so sorry, boys. We'll let you spend some time with her, okay?" a nurse named Carol said, hugging each of us.

"Thanks," I breathed as the medical staff cleared out of the room. We pulled up chairs and sort of sat there in silence, saying a few words and holding her hands. I knew we couldn't stay long. We'd be shifting soon and it was the only time I was actually looking forward to the shift. I could let out my grief wolf form.

After less than an hour, I got up and said, "We need to go."

"I don't wanna leave her," Jordan said, swiping at his tears.

I pulled him to stand and hugged him. "I know, buddy, but we can't stay. They'll take good care of her."

He sobbed into my shoulder, and I just wanted to crumble and fall, but I couldn't. "The moon will help soothe our grief. Let's go."

The drive up the mountain was done in silence, and once we reached our usual spot, I killed the engine and parked the car. Robbie and Jordan bailed out immediately, tearing off their clothes as they went. I wasn't far behind them, and once we reached the clearing, I saw Aunt Becky, Uncle Will and his wife, and my cousins already at the tail end of their shifts.

After stripping off my clothes, I got down on all fours and closed my eyes, trying to calm my breathing. The cries of agony from my brothers floated into my ears and I was grateful, for once, that I didn't have to hear my mom's cries as well. No matter how many times we shifted with her, I could never get used to them. When we were younger, her cry was no different than ours. After dad had died, her cries seemed to come from the depths of her soul, agony radiating out of her. But even then, I refused to feel one day of remorse or sadness for his death. If she hadn't killed him, I was sure she'd have met her death shortly after.

I gritted my teeth as my bones broke and then quickly re-healed into the body of a wolf. My teeth elongating into sharp fangs and my nose and mouth stretching into a wolf happened quickly as black hair sprouted out from everywhere. Once my tail popped out,

I wagged it, and then shook, knowing the tail was the last thing to sprout before I was fully the wolf.

"Where's Sarah?" Uncle Will asked.

"Mom's dead," I said to my aunts and uncle.

"What happened?" Aunt Becky asked before she let out a soulful cry of a howl.

I quickly told them and then ran off into a copse of trees to be alone. I sobbed and cried for my mom, even though no tears came in this form. Conjuring up all I could, I let out a howl as I faced the full moon, letting its healing light bathe me as it took on all my pain and sorrow.

Aunt Becky came up to me and nudged her large white wolf's head against mine, rubbing it in a soothing, motherly way that I needed. We both howled before my aunt, uncle, cousins, and brothers joined us, our wolfish memorial service to our mom who died sad, guilt-ridden, and completely broken.

And it was all my fucking fault.

16

FEELING STABBY
Venom

I knew my time was limited. These motherfuckers were going to cut my heart out. They knew I was a wolf, I heard them talking while in the back of the van they'd thrown me into after I'd awakened from the tranquilizer they'd shot me up with. It wasn't wolfsbane, thankfully, but I knew that was going to come next. Whatever drug they'd stabbed me with only lasted less than ten minutes. Wolfsbane was paralyzing and lasted hours, and I was sure they were saving it for the big finale, not if but when that was going to be.

I was in the back room of a house. Everything around me smelled as if humans inhabited the place. It wasn't the Manchesters' house though, because I'd picked up their scent when Kovah and I had searched it earlier. I suspected this was the third guy's house, and I hoped Face was close to finding out who the hell he was. I was sitting in a chair in some kind of living room. Stone floor with a large dirty throw rug, sofa, TV, and cabinet. The clock on a DVR showed it was 2:30 a.m. The sun would be up in about four hours, and if I had to rely on just Kovah to get me out of here, I was going to be in a world of hurt. He was a ruthless and tough bastard, but I doubted he could take on all three by himself. I also smelled and heard a large dog somewhere, and if I had to guess by the scent, it was probably a Doberman. Those fuckers went for the jugular first and asked questions later.

I looked around the room and tried to find any way of escape or any weapons. There was one small window at the top of one wall I knew I'd never fit out of so that was out of the question. The only way out was through the one and only door. Just then, it opened and I smelled the blood before I saw Lyle coming in holding a red-soaked tissue to his nose. He stalked toward me as I tried desperately to get out of the ropes holding my hands hostage behind me.

"You broke my nose, you mutt," he yelled, backhanding me. My head rocked to the side with a snap.

I growled at him. "Good, now you'll be even uglier."

He slapped me again and I gritted my teeth. *Please, by all means, get me angry, it'll just make me stronger.* "Stop hitting me, you pussy," I said, glaring up at him. "What do you want?"

"Where's the bitch?" he asked, taking the tissue and looking at it before tossing it to the floor. The area around his eyes was already turning black and blue, and he had dried blood all over his bent nose and lips.

I furrowed my brow. "What bitch?"

Leland came through the door and joined us. "The other dog's girlfriend."

"Untie me and I'll take you to her," I lied.

"No, tell us and we won't kill you. Yet. We know you took her to that vampire gang's place you hang out at."

"Well, then I suppose you just answered your own question, Leland." I smirked up at him.

He grabbed a large hunting knife from his belt and jammed it into my thigh. "Don't be a smartass."

I yelled out in pain. "Fuck!"

"Tell us!" he snapped, threatening to twist the knife.

"What do you want with her? She's nobody," I said through gritted teeth.

"She's a witness."

Smiling through my pain, I said, "Uh, she's the least of your problems. We already IDed you Manchester brothers. I'm sure the vamps have a lock on the third thug and are heading here as we speak."

I had no idea if they did, but I had to keep them talking and not torturing.

The brothers looked at each other. "Good, we'll leave your still-beating heart on the porch as a welcome gift."

God, I have got to get that knife out of my thigh. It hurt like a sonofabitch. "Why are you killing wolves?"

Leland sneered. "Because they're unnatural and they kill humans. Just like those undead bloodsuckers. We're coming for them next."

I laughed again. "Good luck with that. They're older, faster, and stronger than you. Not to mention, smarter."

"We've taken a few out before. They're weak when they feed," Lyle said, smiling.

I decided he was the less bright of the two of them, so I kept my attention on him. "So you let them feed on you? You fuck them, too?"

"Only the bitches," Lyle said. "Then, once she's fucked me good, I stab her through the heart and use my Dustbuster to clean up the ashes."

I couldn't tell if he was lying or not, but I had to keep him talking. "Oh really? And where do you meet these female vamps?"

"Oh, here and there. There's a few bars in the Quarter that cater to them. It's worth losing a few ounces of blood for a good fuck and a good kill. In fact, one time…"

He prattled on, but I was getting weak. I was sweating from the pain and the blood running down my pant leg was pooling. I didn't think he'd hit the femoral artery but regardless, I had to get this damn dagger out.

"Could you get me some water?" I asked.

Leland stared at me for a minute and said, "Lyle, go get the dog some water."

Lyle glared at me and went out the door. I wished Leland would go too, because a plan was forming in my head, and I'd never get it executed with him watching me.

"What about some food? Just a piece of fruit or something. I feel sick," I said, looking up at him.

"Hey, Leland, you better get out here, bro!" I heard a voice call. It didn't sound like Lyle's.

He glared at me as if he was contemplating something, and then turned around and disappeared out the door. As soon as it closed and I heard the lock engage, I used the last of my strength to rock the chair from side to side as hard as I could. Finally, the chair tipped over onto its side and I was able to slide my body up so my arms could be free from the chair. The idiots had only tied my hands together, not me to the chair itself.

I stood up, hoping they hadn't heard the chair clatter, and limped over to the short cabinet the TV sat on. Every step was agony, but I had to get out of here. I got down on my knees and used the corner of the wooden cabinet to try to saw through the ropes holding my hands. I shimmied my body up and down as fast as I could to try to loosen the rope. I could hear voices outside the door, along with that dog pacing and panting, and the men seemed to be arguing. I hoped it was a good argument. I needed more time.

I finally felt the rope begin to give and I sawed faster as I yanked my hands apart, hoping to loosen the rope. It eventually gave way, and the first thing I did was yank the dagger from my thigh. Blood gushed out of the wound, and I used a piece of the rope to tie a tourniquet on my thigh like I'd seen in movies. Slow the blood flow, stem the bleeding.

With the dagger in my hand, I leaned down to grab my own knife from my boot, but it was gone. With a head shake, I slowly limped toward the door, waiting for whoever came in first.

17

RESCUE MISSION

Kalissa

My eyes widened as MyAnna led me into the Cobalt Room. A walkway I hadn't even noticed before was set between the clubhouse and the nightclub. It was busy with patrons drinking and having a good time. I wondered how I'd never noticed this club before, but... it wasn't like I went out and partied on the weekends like I had when I was younger. At thirty-three, I mostly stayed home on weekends and read books with Mr. Sparky to keep me company. I realized a long time ago how pathetic it was, but I was completely over finding a husband. Hell, I couldn't even find a boyfriend. Online dating was a joke, and the few guys from work or the coffee shop had been duds. I was convinced there were no good available men left in the world.

Those thoughts immediately conjured up Harlan's face in my mind. Those kind brown eyes, that salt and pepper beard, that rugged haircut, and those lips. My goodness.

"Would you like a drink, Kalissa?" I turned around to see a guy with light brown hair in a ponytail and mischievous eyes talking to me. I remember being introduced to him as one of their "prospects" but of course I couldn't remember his name. His leather vest did not hold a name patch like the others' had.

I cleared my throat and smiled. "Sure, can I get a Diet Coke?"

He smacked his hand on the bar. "Comin' right up." He pulled a glass down from the back of the bar and used the soda gun to pour my drink. He put it on a napkin and slid it over to me. "There ya go. I'm Dash, by the way."

Dash, that's right.

"It's nice to meet you." I lifted my drink and took a sip. It was 2 a.m. and I should be in bed, but clearly these vampires did not sleep at night. I was sure they slept all day, though. If Harlan was a wolf, did he keep their schedule?

Jemini and Jermaine came in with the tablet. She set it on the bar top and we watched as the guys pulled up to an older home in an established neighborhood.

"This is the Manchesters' house. We're gonna kick in the door," Viper said with his face close to the camera. The address is in the group text in case we need backup. I doubt it but stay with us."

I supposed he was talking to us.

"What's going on?" Dash asked.

Jermaine quickly explained.

"Fuck, poor Harlan, man." He shook his head and wiped down the bar.

"I'm confident the guys will get him back," Bloome said before ordering a glass of wine.

I looked back at the tablet, and my mouth dropped open when I saw Shadow disappear into thin air. "Was that a glitch?"

Bloome chuckled. "Oh, he can, uh, I guess you can call it, teleport."

My eyes widened. "You're joking."

She shook her head before putting her lips to the glass. "Nope."

He reappeared quickly. "The house is empty. No signs of any struggle, and certainly no Venom."

"Fuck," Viper said.

"I hate to say it, but we're gonna have to call Psycho. We lost our only bloodhound," Phoenix replied. "And we need to do it quick."

Viper put the phone to his ear. "Sorry to wake you, but we have a fuckin' emergency." Pause. "Okay, meet us at Zombies." Pause.

"See you in ten." He then looked into the camera. "One of you needs to bring me a couple of Harlan's shirts and get down to Zombies. Now."

The screen went blank, and the blue logo came back on.

I looked at the group and Jermaine said, "I'll do it."

"I'm coming with," Jemini said.

"Me too," Bloome said, draining her wine glass

"Me three," I commented.

The twins looked at each other for a minute and said, "Okay, come on."

"Hello, Kalissa. These fuckers treating you okay?" Psycho asked after I'd hugged him.

I laughed. "Yes, just fine. Everyone's been so nice."

He eyed the group then looked at me. "Nobody snackin' on ya or nothin' like that?"

I stared at him in horror and instinctively my hand went to my neck. "Absolutely not."

The vampires laughed.

"Good, now whatcha got?" he asked the group.

Jermaine handed him two shirts he'd taken from Harlan's laundry hamper. Psycho handed one off to another wolf whose name patch read *Jersey*, and they inhaled the shirts deeply.

Psycho said, "Not that I really needed this, but I definitely have his scent now. Do you have any idea where we could start looking?"

"Yes! I got something. Finally!" Face said excitedly, tapping his phone. "I couldn't hack into the postal service's records, so I had to put in an FOI request. I finally got the records from the Manchesters' address to see if anyone else had had mail delivered while they were living there. About six months ago, an Eli Michael Welch, who now resides at 442 Moreau Lane, had mail delivered there temporarily." He looked up from his phone. "I bet that's our guy but I'm going to run a quick background on him. Give me two minutes before we head out." He walked away, tapping some more on his phone.

Admittedly, I was getting more worried by the second. What if these guys had taken Harlan because of me? What if he was seriously hurt—or dead? I heard the vampires say that these hunters had used wolfsbane to incapacitate Donny and Pax before cutting out their hearts. What if that happened to Harlan? His face appeared in my mind again, and I tried to hold back tears. As much as I didn't want to admit it, I was falling hard for the guy and already had feelings that I knew weren't going away. He'd been the nicest man I'd met in, well, forever. The fact that he was an actual werewolf had concerned me, but I'd done it before with Donny and could do it again. They were like human men in some aspects, but for the most part, they were different. Their body temperature was warmer, they, of course, had to leave three days a month to go turn into a wolf, and they were great in bed. I did wonder if that was a wolf thing or maybe Donny had just been that way. Something told me it was a wolf thing, though. I would be lying if I said I hadn't imagined myself underneath Harlan, our sweaty bodies writhing together as he made love to me, over and over…

"Got it!" Face said. "Twenty-nine years old, six-foot-one, one-hundred-ninety pounds. Two priors for assault in New Mexico." He turned the phone around to show us a photo.

"Oh, my God. That's him!" I said, feeling relieved. "He's the one who was with the Manchester guys at the coffee shop."

"You're sure?" Viper, asked, excited.

I nodded. "Absolutely."

He looked at his watch. "Three hours 'til sunup. Let's move."

"Looks like you don't need us, but we're coming, too," Psycho said, heading toward his motorcycle.

"Yes, we might still need you, though," Viper commented as he sprinted toward his motorcycle as well.

I rode in the white van with the twins and Bloome, and it wasn't long until we reached another quiet neighborhood of older homes. The vampires and wolves killed the engines to their motorcycles and parked them along the street. Then, they got into our van and rode with us the two blocks or so to Moreau Street. Jermaine parked the van a couple houses down, and I looked at the unremarkable house. The porch light was on, as were the inside lights. The rest of the neighborhood was dark and quiet due to the hour. I glanced at my phone to see it was past 3 a.m. I was admittedly exhausted, but the adrenaline was keeping me up. I wouldn't sleep until we found Harlan.

"I'll pop in and see what's up," Shadow said.

"Be careful, looks like everyone's awake. Maybe try the backyard first," Phoenix suggested.

"Good idea," Shadow said a second before he fizzled out of existence.

I wasn't the only one who gasped. Psycho and Jersey did as well.

"What the fuck?" Psycho said.

18

BIG EASY BEGINNINGS

New Orleans, LA – 2007

Burying my mother was the final straw. I used it as a lame excuse to break up with Amanda, and that had gone much, much uglier than anticipated. We had been leasing the apartment, so I had to pay her out the ass to keep from having to break the lease. She, of course, went completely apeshit, ranging from crying to screaming to threatening to begging to throwing and breaking some of my stuff. It was extremely hard to leave her, but I knew she wasn't the one for me and didn't see the point in exposing my wolf side to her just to see if maybe she'd accept it.

I decided it was time to leave Colorado. Maybe just temporarily, I wasn't sure. Robbie had gotten married to his wolf girl, and Jordan was dating a wolf himself who was pregnant with his child. I'd gotten them both jobs at the warehouse and where they went from there was up to them. They begged me not to go but I assured them I'd be back someday. I packed what I could and sold what I couldn't, hopped in the Mustang, and just drove. I had always wanted to visit New Orleans, so I thought I'd stop there first, see if I liked it. If not, I would move on. I had a wad of cash I'd saved and planned to live on the road for a while until I found what I was looking for. As of now, I had no idea what that was.

I'd spent some money on a fancy new dash-mounted GPS before I left and that led me straight to the city after an exhausting two-day drive. For now, I decided to check into a cheap motel on the outskirts of the famous city. Unfortunately—or maybe fortunately—unbeknownst to me, I'd arrived a week before the big

Mardi Gras celebration was about to happen. I found this out by listening to people in bars and restaurants talking about it, and by the multiple fliers posted around town and everything in the local paper. I'd had no idea what Mardi Gras even was until I arrived here.

As I flipped through the newspaper, I found myself pausing at the job listings. I saw that dock workers were making a good amount of money and filed that tidbit away in the back of my mind for future reference. No need to go find employment if I hated it here.

After finishing my meal at a small mom-and-pop-type diner, I was anxious to go exploring. I left my car parked in the lot of the diner and took a taxi to the French Quarter to see what all the hype was about.

I had the driver drop me off at the famous old cathedral and from there, I slowly walked along the alleyways that were covered in cobblestone. I found this cool and eclectic. There were multiple shops and food establishments along the way, and the people were very friendly. As darkness set, I literally saw the city come alive. Tourists. Partiers. Happy people everywhere. What else I saw kind of blew my mind. Vampires.

So many fucking vampires.

Growing up in Colorado, I'd rarely run into them. Statistically, the state saw more than three hundred days of sun every year, which made Colorado a less-than-desirable place for the sun-repulsed creatures. I could count on one hand the number of times I'd met one—and those encounters never got violent. They'd go their way, and we'd go ours.

But here? Holy shit, the place was teeming with them. I'd ordered a drink in each bar to sort of survey the scene, and at every single place I'd spotted at least one. I recalled the classic book-turned-movie about the origins of vamps being here, but thought it was a myth or urban legend. Turned out, it wasn't. It seemed the night creatures craved the rich, old history, the almost seemly constant cloud cover, and access to the abundance of human tourists to satisfy their hunger. What I didn't see, however, were any wolves.

Being one myself, I could see why. We desired cold climates and access to a clear night where the full moon could be gazed upon, its light giving us power and helping us to heal. The mountainous region where I used to shift was at least eight thousand feet above sea level, and most of the year, except for a few rain and snow showers, the sky in Colorado was clear and the air was fresh and clean.

Still... there was something magical about this city. I wasn't set on going back to Colorado anytime soon, and the nearness of the water of the Mississippi River was something different—and I liked it. It had me thinking I should probably stay here a while and see what else the city could offer. I had always had an affination to water, regardless of being a wolf, and as I strolled along the bank of the Mississippi, I watched the large paddleboats bob on the water, the laughs and voices from their partygoers floating along the air and into my ears.

"It's not every day you see a wolf in these parts."

I turned quickly, immediately defensive, toward the voice. A man I sensed as a wolf sat on a park bench staring out at the water. I slowly approached him. Stopping about five feet away, I said, "I noticed that myself."

"New to town?" he asked, still not looking at me but staring out at the dark waters of the river.

"You could say that." I shoved my hands into the pockets of my leather jacket. The cold had never really bothered me, but there was something about this humid night air that was strangely different.

"I would avoid the Quarter if I were you. Lots of vamps." The man looked to be in his late forties and crossed one leg over the other.

"I noticed," I replied. "Seems the city is chock full of them."

"It is the city's legacy, after all," he replied. Then, he finally looked at me. "I'm Zach Monroe, by the way."

I dipped my head at him. "I'm Harlan Lahey. Nice to meet you."

"Unfortunately, since there aren't a lot of us around here, we don't really have a pack or any kind of leadership here, so I hope you didn't come here looking for one."

"I didn't," I replied quickly. "I was just checking out the city. I'm from Colorado, but it was time to leave."

"Sounds like you're running from something."

I shrugged and walked toward him slowly. "Eh, I wouldn't say that. Just needing a fresh start." It was a half-truth. I was going to miss my brothers and cousins but certainly not Amanda or the constant memories of the horrors I'd been through over the past six years.

"I see," he said.

"So, where do you shift around here?" I asked, glad I'd met another wolf because where to shift was rapidly becoming my first concern.

"There are no basements here, the city actually sits below sea level, so the ground is too unstable. There are abandoned warehouses and such. Or you can drive out to the country and fend for yourself against the other wild animals."

It had never occurred to me to shift in the basement. We'd always run free on the full moons. I supposed if a wolf couldn't control himself, he'd be chained and caged. Sounded awful.

"Okay, but where do *you* shift?" I repeated.

He stood, his hands in his pockets. "I own one of the warehouses. You're welcome to use it, come shift with us."

"I thought you said there were no packs around here."

He chuckled, his eyes crinkling at the corners. He raked his hand over his beard. "We don't. It's just me, my wife, and my son."

"Very kind of you, I'll give it some thought. Any way you could give me directions to the more secluded nature-type areas? I don't mind fighting off a few wildcats."

He chuckled. "Sure, just drive north for about an hour. You'll see the landscape thin out and the buildings get smaller and smaller."

I put my hand out to shake. "Thanks."

Zach looked down at it, then took it, pumping it up and down. "No problem, Harlan."

"Could I get your number? Maybe we could go for a beer sometime. Could use some friends," I said with more boldness than I felt.

"Sure, sure." He pulled out his phone. "What's your number?"

I recited it and then received a text from him. "Thank you," I said, holding it up.

"Well, I'm gonna go see if the missus has cooled off yet." He chuckled. "I'll be in touch for that beer."

"Good luck," I replied as he walked off.

Two weeks later, I found myself getting hired on the spot down at the docks. They only had the graveyard shift available, and I again made up a religious excuse as to why I would need three nights a week off. He was suspicious of my excuse but told me that would be fine, but they'd be unpaid days off. I assured him that was all right, and if those days fell on one or both of my days off, I'd be at work as usual after.

I quickly noticed that about a quarter of the graveyard-shift employees were vampires. Remarkably, I had no problems at all with them. They just wanted to do their eight and then hit the gate, not start drama at work. They knew I was a wolf, and generally left me alone. I'd been raised to believe these creatures were our natural-born enemies, but that wasn't my observation at all. I knew what they were capable of, but I figured if they were working honest jobs, they couldn't be the murderous, bloodthirsty troublemakers I'd believed them to be my whole life.

The job was hard work, but I was building up my physique and was glad I didn't need to waste time and money on a gym. I got enough of a workout during these eight hours.

One night, as I was clocking in, I noticed a new guy—tall, red hair, looked fairly young, and had a terrible sense of style.

"How you doing?" I asked him as he put gloves on and rolled up his sleeves. "Harlan."

"Gabe," he replied, shaking my hand.

Vampire.

Not that it mattered, like I'd said. We slid into an easy conversation about generic things like the weather and things to do in the city, and then when the whistle blew, he asked if he could spend his lunch break with me. I found this odd because the rest of the vamps spent theirs together since they didn't eat.

I shrugged. "Sure."

As I ate, he asked about my family and where I was from and I told him bits and pieces, leaving out the stuff about my parents. I didn't want to talk about it and didn't think I ever would.

Every night for the next few months, Gabe and I spent our lunch breaks together, talking about motorcycles, politics, the weather, and everything in between.

As we were getting off of work one morning, the sky was still dark as we headed to our bikes. As Gabe was about to put on his helmet, this man appeared out of nowhere it seemed. He must have not seen me because he crept up behind Gabe with a humongous machete in his hand.

I'd never run so fast. "Gabe, look out!" I yelled. Quickly, I tackled the guy to the ground and sat on him, punching him in the face. His machete went flying.

"What the fuck do you think you're doing?" I snapped, my fist poised over his face.

Gabe stared down at us, wide-eyed.

"He was about to take your head off, man," I told my friend.

"Is that so?" Gabe asked him. "And who the hell are you?"

"Watch out, I'm not the only hunter around, leech," he jeered, a smug look on his face.

"Fuck this," I muttered under my breath. I looked around the lot briefly to see we were alone and then twisted his neck until it broke, and he went lifeless under me.

Gabe thanked me sincerely and we had a discussion about what to do with the body as he helped me up. We agreed we had to dump it into the water. As we were about to do so, we heard a voice.

"Need some help?"

Gabe and I turned around. Where a few seconds ago there was nobody, now stood two big bikers in leather vests and boots.

"Who the fuck are you?" I asked, still shaking from having just killed a man.

They were across the parking lot one second, then the next they were standing in front of us.

Vampires.

They introduced themselves but their names were on their vests.

The blond one said, "You're a wolf."

I nodded.

"You saved a vampire from a hunter. Why did you do that?" the other one, Shadow, asked. Damn the guy was tall.

I explained that Gabe was not only my coworker, but my friend.

Viper put his hand out to shake, and I reciprocated. His hand was cold. He explained that they were following the hunter.

They offered to help us dump the body but suggested we burn it first. I also thought that was a good idea. Shadow pulled a lighter from his pocket, but Gabe told him to put it away. Then, my friend did something that blew my mind. He ignited a fireball in his fist out of thin air. There were no matches or an incinerator. He tossed the fire at the hunter's body, and it went up in flames.

The vampires seemed to be as shocked as I was. Shadow asked how he did it.

"Took the words right out of my mouth," I replied, staring wide-eyed at my friend.

He quickly explained how his little talent had appeared after being cursed by a witch. He'd told me his incredible story earlier. Combined with the fact that that Shadow guy could disappear into thin air and then reappear elsewhere, combined with Gabe's fire trick, I had no idea vampires could do anything special besides not age and hypnotize people.

Gabe and I dumped the body into the water. I kept the machete. It was wicked sharp, and I'd always wanted one.

As I got on my bike, I heard the bikers tell Gabe they were going to meet him tomorrow night during our lunch break. I wondered what they wanted with my friend.

19

HEALING HANDS

Venom

I almost fell over when Shadow appeared next to me just as I was about to hide behind the door to lie in wait for whoever would come in. "Thank fuck you're here!"

"I saw you through the window." He pointed to the window at the top of the wall. Of course he'd been tall enough to see through it. "I smell blood, lots of it," he continued, looking me over and spotting my bloodied thigh. "What the hell?"

"Fucker stabbed me," I said quietly, holding up the hunting knife.

"Do you know how many there are?" he asked.

I nodded, bracing myself on the wall. I was starting to feel dizzy. "At least three. And a dog. Doberman, I'd guess."

"You find out why they snatched you?" he asked, helping me to the sofa to sit.

"They want Kalissa. They warned her to stay away from wolves and she didn't. Guess they think she's a liability since she can ID them." I took a deep breath. "I told them it was already too late. I think they're just idiots."

He snorted. "I don't think, I know."

"How'd you find me?" I asked.

He glanced up the stairs and said, "Face checked the Manchesters' address to see who else had lived there. Third guy named Eli popped up from a few months ago. This is his current address."

"Smart," I murmured. "I don't think this tourniquet is working. Gonna need some stitches, I think. I won't heal that fast unless I can shift, but the full moon's not for another week."

"I'll be right back. Hang tight." He disappeared.

I felt weak and out of control and did not like that. I wasn't sure I could fight like this and that concerned me. I could only hope they brought the calvary—which I had no doubt they had. I also wondered if Kalissa was safe at the clubhouse. I'd said these hunters were idiots, but I wouldn't put it past them to have more help around, trying to break into the clubhouse somehow. If I was them, I'd go through Cobalt Room, but we always had a prospect guarding the walkway between it and the clubhouse. My worry about her increased when I thought about someone hurting her. We'd offered her protection and now that was at risk.

A loud crash, shouting, and a dog barking wildly echoed from outside the door. With the dagger in my hand, I ambled toward the door, each step agony in my thigh. I tried the doorknob but of course it was locked. I was too weak now to try to snap it off.

I banged on it. "Get me out of here!"

It was opened by Phoenix several seconds later who pulled me into a one-armed hug. "Thank God." He looked down at my leg. "Fuck. Can you walk?"

I nodded and he helped me walk through the kitchen, where the body of Lyle lay with his throat ripped out and his eyes staring blankly at nothing. On the living room floor lay Leland with his head twisted at an unnatural angle, his lifeless eyes also open along with his mouth in a silent scream. A third man, I'm assuming Eli, was still alive. Viper, Shadow, Face, and Psycho were towering over him.

They turned around when they saw me.

"I smell blood," Psycho said, looking at my leg.

I held up the dagger. "Hurts like a sonofabitch."

Psycho slapped Eli upside his head. "You do that?"

"Fuck you, dog." He cleared his throat and then spat a wad of saliva at Psycho's chest.

Phoenix grabbed Eli's hair and craned his head back. "The man asked you a question. You spit again and we'll rip your tongue out."

"No, I didn't. Lyle or Leland must have."

"Why did you take Venom?" Viper asked.

Eli glared at us. "I'm done talking. Just kill me."

"Is that what you want?" I asked. "Why don't you just tell them you took me to get to the girl?"

"Fuck off, mutt," he said to me.

I shook my head. "I need to take care of this," I said to Phoenix, pointing at my leg. Can you take me back to the clubhouse? I'll stitch it up myself."

"We'll meet you back there," Viper informed us.

As Phoenix helped me toward the door, every step agony, I suddenly remembered something. I looked at the guys. "Where's the Doberman?"

Psycho took a can of dip from his back pocket and pulled out a pinch. "Demon brought my truck over. We're takin' her back to our clubhouse. She'll be a great guard dog."

"A guard dog for dogs," Eli said, laughing.

Psycho punched him in the face.

"Asshole!" Eli snapped, holding his nose.

As Phoenix led me out of the house, I limped down the walkway and heard rapid footsteps. I looked up to see Kalissa running toward me, fear and relief on her face.

She wrapped her arms around me, and I winced as her leg bumped mine. "Oh, my God. I'm so glad you're all right!"

I hugged her back and saw Jemini run into Phoenix's arms. He kissed her and then Bloome came up behind them. "Where's Shadow?"

"Inside, interrogating," I said with a smirk.

She ran up the steps toward the door. I was going to warn her about the macabre scene inside, but I was too weak.

Kalissa smoothed my hair back from my forehead and looked into my face. "What's wrong? Are you in pain?"

I nodded. "It'll be fine. Just need some stitches."

She looked down at my leg. "Oh, God. You guys got a medical kit or anything at the clubhouse?"

"No," Jemini said. "I keep telling them they need to get one, in case we have humans there."

"I have one at my house," Kalissa said. "If you guys can drive us there." She looked at Jemini.

"Sure," Jemini said. "Let's go."

"You know, if you can't put in stitches, I can. I've done it before," I said to Kalissa.

She smacked me in the chest. "Of course I can. Now, give me your belt." She helped me slide it off and then she buckled it tight around the top of my thigh.

I hobbled into her small house, and her cat immediately came out to greet her, and again it hissed at me when it saw me.

"Oh, stop it, Mr. Sparky. He's not going to hurt you."

The cat sat a safe distance away, watching us.

"Take off your pants and sit here," Kalissa told me, pulling out a chair.

I nodded as she disappeared into the back of the house.

Slowly kicking off my boots and socks, I undid the belt and

dropped it to the floor, then painfully pulled my pants down. The blood had glued the denim to my leg, and I hissed as I had to peel them down.

"Shit. I could have just cut them away. I'm sorry," she said, coming toward me holding a red bag with a white cross on it. She unzipped it and laid out the contents on the table.

At least I'd worn my nice boxers today, I mused to myself when she got down on her knees to inspect the wound in my thigh.

She cleaned it off with a warm rag before using what I assumed was alcohol by the way it burned to disinfect it.

"I'm sorry," she said when I sucked in a breath.

"It's fine," I said. "I'd rather not get an infection."

Once it was cleaned enough, she inspected the wound. "You know, it's not as bad as I thought, especially for a stab wound."

"I heal faster than humans, but not as fast as vampires," I said, not knowing what else to say. Having her hands and face that close to my dick was uncomfortable because it wasn't meant to be sexual, and I was having inappropriate thoughts.

"I see," she said. "And how fast do vampires heal?" She pulled out a small pair of scissors and some sutures.

"Wicked fast. Like, this cut would be gone, not even a scar by now if it had happened to a vamp."

"Wow, no wonder they don't need medical supplies at their place," she said. Then she looked up at me. "Sorry I don't have anything to numb this with."

"It's fine, just do it," I replied.

It only took about ten stitches, and it wasn't even that painful. I knew the wound would heal before the stitches needed to come out, so I'd just cut them out myself in a couple of days. She put a bandage around my leg and taped it up.

"Okay, good to go," she said, seeming proud of herself. "Hopefully you're not in too much pain?" she asked as she stood. "I have some Tylenol here." She held up a packet.

"Nah, I'm all right. I don't think those pants are gonna go back on though," I said, pointing to my bloody jeans on the floor.

"Probably not," she said.

"If you don't mind, I'll have one of the guys bring me some pants and then I'll be out of your hair."

"Don't be silly. It's late. Just stay here and I'll drive you back to your clubhouse tomorrow sometime." She was now sitting in a chair next to me. She grabbed my hand. "I'd like it if you stayed."

"Okay, you twisted my arm," I mused, now feeling nervous. Was she inviting me to sleep on her couch or in her bed? I looked at my watch: 4:29 a.m. "Well, it's already tomorrow and I do need some rest."

She helped me to stand. "Come on."

I limped down the hallway and she told me to sit on the bed. Then, she removed my cut and pulled my shirt off over my head, leaving me in just my boxers. I stared curiously at her to see how stripped down she planned to get. She didn't disappoint. Soon, she stood in just a pair of lacy blue underwear and a matching bra. She was very thin—I could see her hipbones and a couple ribs—and I wanted to ask her about what Jemini had mentioned to me but decided against it. She wasn't unattractive by any means. I was just worried about her.

She pulled the covers back and instructed me to get in. I obeyed, and then she crawled in next to me. Her cat meowed what I assumed was a protest to me taking his spot, but she just told him to get into his cat bed set near the bathroom door, and he obeyed.

I didn't have the heart to tell her I was starving, but I'd seen the inside of her fridge and knew we'd be stopping somewhere tomorrow on the way back to the clubhouse for food.

The blood loss and general excitement from the night had me exhausted. As soon as Kalissa laid her head on my chest, I pulled her tightly to me as she draped her leg over my good one. With her warm body wrapped around mine, we fell quickly fell asleep.

20

PIERCINGS & OYSTERS
Kalissa

I woke up to a very warm body pressed against my back. Blinking my eyes open, I saw strong hands wrapped around me. I also felt a hard erection pressed against my tailbone.

"Good morning," Harlan said in my ear, his voice husky and low.

I rolled over and looked up at him. His light-brown eyes stared into mine as he brushed some hair out of my face. "Good morning." I glanced at the bedside clock. "Well, good afternoon."

He chuckled and leaned down, kissing me softly on the lips. He felt so good, and it had been so long since I'd been with anyone. I instinctively pressed my body into his as I kissed him back. I felt his hand go around my back and unclasp my bra. We broke apart briefly so I could slide it off.

Harlan looked down at my breasts. "So beautiful." Then, he kissed me again.

We seemed to be moving in slow motion, not urgent or in a hurry to get to the main event. I enjoyed the relaxed foreplay, and it was turning me on so much. I wanted nothing more than for him to rip my panties off and slam himself into me. Reaching down, I slid his boxers down his legs and he wiggled out of them. I noticed a barbell-type piercing on the underside of the biggest penis I'd ever seen, near the head. Interesting, I'd never been with a guy who had one. Intrigued and excited, I gently pushed him on his back, careful to mind his leg. I also shimmied out of my underwear and sat on his pelvis, running my hands over his chest. He had a nice smattering of chest hair, the perfect amount. I found it sexy as hell. I ran my finger over the large bird tattoo on his neck. I noticed he didn't have any other tats, though, just that one.

"You want to do this, darlin'?" he asked, running his hands over my waist and then gripping my hips. "You want me inside you?"

I nodded, chewing my lip. "Yes, more than anything."

He reached down and ran his finger over my wet slit, then pushed it inside me. I craned my head back and moaned. "Yes."

"Fuck, you're soaked, darlin'." He rubbed circles on my clit, and I groaned, my nipples pebbling in response. The more he stroked me, the more I began to tremble, feeling the climax building. Once he reached up and rolled his fingers around my nipple, my breaths sped up and I bucked my hips, willing the orgasm to come faster as he massaged my sensitive spot over and over, using my slick juices to work his finger magic.

My whole body shook violently as I came hard. "Harlan!"

"So fucking beautiful," he said, pulling his finger out and sucking on it.

I lifted myself up to my knees and lined up his dick with my dripping core. "I'm clean and on the pill," I said right before I impaled myself on him.

I sucked in a breath of pain as he stretched me wide, but it was quickly replaced with a delicious pleasure, and we groaned in unison. When our bodies began to move in sync, it was like we were made for each other. He used one hand to grip my hip, and the other to run his fingertips gently over my rock-hard nipple. We found a rhythm that had both of us moving faster and faster, his cock ramming up into me over and over, that piercing on his dick igniting something delicious and erotic inside of me I'd never felt before. I partially stood, my feet flat on the bed so we could watch our connection together. He slid his finger over my clit, and I put my hand over his, touching us both as we ground together.

When his movements began to get faster and faster, I felt that pressure low in my belly building up again. Between his magic fingers and the movement of his cock piercing touching just the right spot, I crashed over the edge again, crying out while shaking with an earth-shattering orgasm that made me see stars behind my closed lids.

"Fuck!" he grunted, stilling his hips and exploding inside of me, both of us moaning and panting like we'd just run a marathon.

I collapsed against his chest, trying to catch my breath. He ran a hand over my hair and said, "That was incredible."

I could only nod. We lay there for a few minutes until he pulled out of me. I hopped up and went to the bathroom to clean up, and once that was done, I brought him back a towel.

"Thanks," he said, wiping himself off and tossing the towel to the floor. "Get your fine ass back in bed," he demanded.

I jumped onto the bed like a kid and giggled when he pulled me into his arms and kissed my head. "That was fucking amazing."

"I thought so," I agreed. "Harlan… I hope you don't think that I… that I, like, do this a lot. Because I don't."

He grabbed my jaw so I had to look up at him. "Hey, I didn't think that at all. We're just two consenting adults attracted to each other. To be honest, I've been avoiding women and relationships in general. You're the first woman who's even piqued my interest in a very long time."

This warmed my insides. "Really?"

"Yes, really. I know you just lost your boyfriend, and I feel bad about that. I hope you know I would never take advantage of you. If you want this to be a one-time thing, I wouldn't like it, but I would respect whatever you wanted."

I quickly shook my head. "No, I don't want that. Truth is, I've been lonely. Mr. Sparky can only offer so much company."

As if on cue, the cat meowed.

"Yeah, I'll feed you in a minute," I replied to him.

"I feel the same way about the Nighthawks. Most of them are coupled up now anyway. It's been hard to watch them all find love, knowing I never would."

I lightly raked my fingernails over his chest. "Sometimes it takes a while to find the right person. I'm no spring chicken either. I thought Donny was it, but now that I've met you, I know he wasn't. It was never like this with him."

He pulled me tight. "I hope we can explore this further, then."

"I'd like that."

"But, for now, it seems Mr. Sparky isn't the only one who needs food. Let's shower and go get some grub."

"You probably need to find some pants first," I teased.

"Shit," he said. "Well, your car is here, right? We'll stop by the store, you can run in and grab me a pair, then, we eat."

I told myself to stay calm. I wasn't particularly hungry but knew I should eat something. So far, Harlan hadn't really said anything, but I knew if I was going to get serious with him, he'd need to know about my problem. Just not today. Today seemed like it was going to be a great day.

It was almost dinnertime by the time we got to the Quarter, and he suggested seafood. I thought that sounded good.

"How do the jeans fit?" I asked as we were seated.

He looked down and grinned. "They're a little tight, but it's okay."

I waggled my eyebrows at him. "You look more than okay in them."

He chuckled and ran his fingers over his beard before setting his menu down. "You're so damn cute. Where've you been all my life?"

I felt a blush steal across my cheeks, and I shrugged. "Oh, I've been here. We just got lucky our paths crossed when they did."

Harlan stared at me for a long time.

"What?" I asked.

"You have the most beautiful blue eyes. Like sapphires."

I blushed again. "Thanks. So do you. So unique."

Suddenly, they flashed yellow, then went back to brown. My eyes widened. "How did you do that?"

"It's a wolf thing, darlin'."

Donny's eyes had never done that, but I didn't want to bring him up, so I said, "Oh, that's pretty cool." I lowered my voice and looked around the restaurant before asking, "So what color is your wolf when you turn?"

"Black with a gray beard, just like me." He beamed a smile at me.

I laughed. "Seriously?"

"Yep," he said, then looked down at his menu. "I don't know about you, but I'm starving."

"I could eat," I said.

"What are you going to have?" he asked.

I shrugged. "I'll have whatever you're having."

"You like chargrilled oysters?" he asked.

"I honestly have never tried them, but it sounds good," I replied truthfully. I only ate out on my lunch breaks because I only ate once a day, but I wasn't going to tell him that. Donny was always pushing me to eat, and I knew Harlan would be the same way. All guys were.

The server came and took our orders, and he ordered two dozen chargrilled oysters and a cup of sausage gumbo soup.

"Do you want any wine or anything?" he asked.

I shook my head. "No, just water, thank you."

He ordered a beer. "My stomach's gnawin' on my backbone," he said. "I don't think I've eaten since yesterday morning."

"They didn't feed you, those kidnappers?" I asked.

He shook his head. "No, but I wasn't there very long before the calvary showed up."

"I'm just glad we got there when we did. That Face guy, he's pretty good with computers and hacking into stuff, huh?" I asked.

"Yeah, the guy's not just a pretty face, I'll tell you that. He's very young so he's good with all the computer stuff," Harlan said as the server set down his beer.

"What do you mean young? I mean—" I paused, waiting for the server to be far enough away—"I know vampires don't get old and he does look very young, but isn't he frozen that way?" I asked.

He lifted the bottle to his lips. "Yes, but he's not even twenty-five I don't think. Only got turned a couple years ago."

"I see. I'd love to hear everyone's stories one of these days," I said. "Which one's the oldest?"

"In actual years, Gabe. Uh, Phoenix. He's over 180 years old."

My eyes widened. "No way, I bet he has a lot of cool stories."

He chuckled. "Not really, he spent 150 of those years in some kind of magical coma. I'll let him tell you about it. Well, that new guy, Andy, he's the same age as Gabe too, but I haven't gotten the chance to talk to him. But... in physical years, I'm the oldest. Well, I'm not a vampire. Vane's like thirty, I think."

"How old are you?" I asked, realizing I'd told him my age a few days ago but I hadn't asked his. Judging by the gray in his hair and beard, I knew he was older than me.

"I'm thirty-nine. I'll be forty in a few months."

I made a purring sound with my tongue. "Mmm silver fox. Sexy."

He chuckled after taking a sip of his beer. "You think so? I thought about getting some of that dye stuff for my beard, what's it called? To get rid of the gray. I'm gonna look like grandpa next to all those young vamps here soon."

"Don't you dare," I said, meaning it. "You're sexy as hell. I'll prove it to you again later." I winked at him. "Can I call you Daddy?"

He narrowed his eyes at me, but I could tell he was biting back a smile. "Only if you want to get spanked."

Wow, I was being bold. I was never this forward with men, but there was something about Harlan that made me want to make sure he knew how much I was falling for him and that I didn't want to let him go. A shiver ran down my spine at the thought of getting spanked by him. *Sounds like fun.*

The oysters arrived and I ate three of them. They were delicious.

A PLACE TO BELONG

New Orleans, LA – 2008

After Gabe quit the dock job to join the Nighthawks, I was admittedly a little bummed out. He was the most genuine friend I'd made since I'd moved here. I had gone out for beers with Zach a few times, but for the most part, I shifted out in the woods by myself every month. There were other wolves around, but we didn't really socialize outside of the shifting. I began to wonder if I shouldn't just tuck my tail between my legs and move back home to Colorado. I couldn't deny that I missed my brothers. Jordan's daughter was born last year, and he constantly sent me pictures. She had blonde hair that stuck straight up off her head and his brown eyes. She was adorable and I wanted to meet her. He'd married the child's mother and I missed being at that milestone as well.

Gabe did keep in touch, and sometimes we met for coffee or whatever, but he was busy with his club. When he told me about what they did, I found it fascinating. He'd been there six months and had told me at our last coffee meeting that he was going to push for them to let me join. Living in a den of vampires did not sound like the most ideal situation for a wolf, but I was growing bored and lonely in this city, and if I didn't find something besides a stupid job to ground me here, I was probably going to go exploring again. I wondered if Florida would be nice to live in. Fewer vampires there, I was sure. Not that I had anything against the sunlight-resistant, blood-drinking creatures. They'd always been nice to me.

I was just closing up my Igloo after eating my lunch, knowing the whistle was about to blow.

"Harlan!"

I turned to see Gabe, Viper, and Shadow standing at the end of the dock.

I headed toward them. "Hey, guys. Everything okay?"

Viper nodded and shook my hand. "Yes, and I'll cut straight to the point. You want in the Nighthawks?"

I glanced at Gabe, who smiled at me and nodded his head a little in encouragement.

"What would I have to do?" I asked.

"Keeping it one hundred percent real, we could use a member who could go out in the daylight," Shadow said.

I looked up at him. "So, an errand boy?" I chuckled.

"Not at all." Viper shook his head. "Sometimes shit comes up that we can't handle because they happen during business hours. Or there's a threat at our door that we can't risk fighting because it's during the day. That hunter y'all killed out here a few months ago? He'd been trying to find a way into the clubhouse in the middle of a bright, sunny day. Caught him on our cameras. It would have been nice to have someone around who could have gone out there and shanked his ass."

Murder? "Wow, so you would have just had him killed for sneaking around your warehouse?"

"No, we would have, ah, interrogated him first, "Shadow replied. "Would have been cool to have someone to go outside and snatch him up, though."

I put my hands on my hips and looked at the three of them. "So, that's all you need from me? What do I get in return?"

"No, we'll need your loyalty and commitment. You fight with us if we need you to. We have each other's backs. In return, you live at our clubhouse in Shreveport. We'll eventually be moving it down here, so we'll need help with that, as well. Quit your job, move up there with us. Free room and board and a cell phone. You already have a bike, so that's good. You'll just need your own dough for whatever you like to spend money on. Besides, Phoenix here won't shut up about recruiting you."

"Yeah, guilty as charged," he replied with a grin, and I noticed his name patch read *Phoenix*. How appropriate.

I literally had nothing here except the job. What did I have to lose? I didn't really trust Viper and Shadow implicitly, but I trusted Gabe and I knew he wouldn't do anything that would put me in harm's way. "Okay, I'll do it."

"Yes!" Gabe said, punching the air.

Viper shook my hand. "See you tomorrow night. Phoenix will text you the address."

I nodded and they walked off. As they were heading toward their bikes, Gabe turned around, stuck his tongue out, and made the sign of the devil with his fingers, a huge grin on his face.

I shook my head, trying not to smile. Goofy bastard.

Of course, the first thing I noticed upon entering the Nighthawks' clubhouse were the huge cells, or cages located off to the left.

"The hell are those for?" I asked Viper as he was showing me around.

"Rogue wolves," he replied. With my sharp eyesight, I noticed some dried blood on the floor and the bars.

"You kill them?" I asked.

Phoenix shook his head. "No, but we've had them get... unruly."

"Where do you shift?" Viper asked me.

"Right now, I head into the woods during the night and go back to my apartment during the day."

He looked at Shadow. "If you stay with us, we're going to ask that you stay in one of those at night. It's not that we don't trust you, it's just that—"

"We don't trust you," Shadow finished for him.

I looked at them incredulously. "You're joking."

"No, man. Sorry," Viper said. "It's for your protection and ours. Just until we build trust between us."

"I'm perfectly civil during my shifts. I'm aware of my surroundings. I don't attack unless I feel threatened," I said, starting to get pissed off. Thank fuck I hadn't quit my job yet. Today and tomorrow were my days off and I'd planned on giving my notice on Monday.

"Just until we build trust," Gabe reassured me, his hand on my shoulder. "Once that happens, Viper will make you lieutenant. Right, V?"

I looked at the Nighthawks' leader as he replied, "Absolutely. Prove your dedication and we'll reward you."

I could see his point. If I were in his shoes, I'd probably do the same thing. But spending all night in a cage? Ugh. "Fine, for the first month, but after that, all bets are off."

"Who knows, you may like it in there. We'll get you whatever you want to eat," Phoenix said.

"It's not about food," I argued. "I need to roam free when I'm the wolf. Be under the full moon. It's how our bodies heal."

"Heal from what?" Shadow asked.

I chose my words carefully. "If we're sick or injured."

"But as long as you're healthy, you'll be all right in here?" Shadow asked, pointing to the cells.

Technically, he was right, but it was hard to explain how I needed the moon's light to heal me emotionally too. No fucking way was I going to get into that, though. "Fine."

Viper smiled. "All right, come with me."

I followed him across the warehouse to an office, where he produced a leather vest. "Here's your cut."

Holding it up, I could see the name patch read *Venom*. I chuckled a little. "I guess *Wolf* or *Dog* would have been too obvious?" Admittedly, during the four-plus hour drive up here, I'd wondered what kind of club name they'd give me.

"Pretty much. We know wolves have venom in their bite, and while I was trying to stay away from the snake theme, it seemed to fit in this situation. You don't bite us, and we won't bite you. You dig?" Viper asked.

"I dig," I replied with a smile, shrugging on the cut. "Fits like a glove."

"Welcome to the club, Venom," Viper replied with a handshake.

"Thanks," I said, feeling a sort of pride begin to seep into my soul. I'd never belonged to anything but my own biological family, which had been fucked up pretty much my whole life. This felt different. This felt like family. Like home.

"Now, if you're up for it, let's take you to see Jax and get you tatted," Viper said.

"Oh! The bird. Hell yes," I said.

As we walked toward the door, Phoenix pointed to his arm. "Since your guns aren't as big as mine, I don't suggest you copy me."

I punched him in his "gun" and said, "Fuck off, fireboy. I'm getting a neck tat."

"Bad-ass!" He fist-bumped me.

"Hey, does anyone at the shop do piercings, too?" I asked.

"I do recall a piercing area there," Viper said. "Why, gonna get you a nose ring or something?"

I waggled my eyebrows. "No, this one is going to be for the ladies."

Phoenix and Viper groaned as we headed toward our bikes to see Jax.

22

GOODBYES

Venom

A few days later, as we sat in church, I could tell by the look on Viper's face that he had bad news. I sipped a beer and waited for Ally to bring me the burger I'd ordered from the food truck next door.

Kovah stood next to Viper with his hands behind his back, a solemn look on his face where normally there was a smug grin or some sort of smartass smirk. Andy, the newest prospect of the Nighthawks, stood on the other side.

Viper pounded the gavel. "I'll cut straight to the chase… Kovah here is leaving us. His wife's job is moving them to New York, and he's chosen to move with her. Which is regrettable, but understandable."

"I'm never *not* going to be a Nighthawk," Kovah quickly added. "You guys took me in when you could have killed me." He laughed, and I recalled the story he'd told me about how he was spying on them for the BSI and how Viper almost killed him. "I'll be back to visit. I love this fucking city. She embraced me when I was alone, and the people of the Big Easy made me feel alive when I just wanted to die after having to start over."

"Aren't you from New York?" Dash asked as he poured a drink for Face.

He looked at the prospect and nodded. "Yes, Rochester. That's upstate. The DOJ is stationing Manta in New York City. I may pop upstate and see how my siblings and nieces and nephews are doing." If I could have seen his eyes behind his sunglasses, I would have thought he'd winked at Dash.

"I've got to replace Kovah with a new lieutenant. I'm going to nominate Andy here, but we need to take it to a vote."

"Aren't there other prospects who are in line before the new guy?" Paz, a prospect, called out.

"Yeah, but Andy's got a law degree, so he kind of cuts in line. Nighthawks need good legal representation."

"I vote yes," Face said, lifting the club soda to his mouth. I knew it wasn't water because it fizzed and he didn't drink alcohol, ever.

"He's got my vote!" Phoenix said, raising his hand.

"Me too," I called out.

"Well, Shadow and I already approve. Welcome, Andy. We'll get you a club name soon. Yours has been the hardest to choose so far."

Kovah lifted his beer to his lips. "A legal eagle. Nice."

Viper looked at Kovah and turned his head. "Eagle. Huh. That might work."

Andy's blue eyes crinkled at the corners as he smiled, his jet-black hair and short beard glowing blue under the lights of the club. He grabbed the lapels of his suit jacket, tugging on them. "Eagle. I like it."

"I'm gonna sleep on it," Viper said. Then he turned to Kovah. "Thanks for ten great years. Please come back and visit." They hugged and I felt a little nostalgic. As annoying as the hybrid could be, he had made me laugh on more than one occasion, and he was a serious badass with a dagger. I'd seen him take down wolves and the occasional succubus without a second thought. I'd listened to his story once and had no doubt as to why he was half out of his mind. His turning into a vampire had been halted by the one who'd turned him, which had caused him to become a hybrid. I didn't think any of us—vampire, wolf, witch, or otherwise—particularly loved what we were, but at least we knew what we were and where we belonged. Kovah had drifted for years, unsure where he belonged. I was glad he'd found his wife.

"I'm gonna miss you fuckers for real. Next round's on me." He lifted his drink and we all clapped.

Yep, I'd miss the fucker.

I felt warm arms wrap around my waist and I turned around to see Kalissa looking up at me.

"Hi," I said, smoothing some hair away from her face. "Having fun?"

"Yep. Everyone's so nice. I'm glad you convinced me to stay. But since those guys are dead, I guess I'll go back home. Will you visit me there?"

I grabbed her hand and kissed it. "I don't want you to leave just yet. I like having you here, darlin'."

She chewed her lip and looked up at me through her lashes. "I admit I like it here too. You keep me warm at night."

"See? You need someone to warm up those freezing cold feet of yours. If you move back home, you'll have to sleep in socks. That won't be any fun."

"You do have a point, Mr. Lahey." She leaned up and kissed me on the lips briefly.

I heard a few whistles and looked around to see Kovah, Face, Shadow, and Bloome looking at us with knowing looks on their faces.

I flipped them off and they all laughed.

"You can stay here as long as you want," I said, my attention back on the beautiful blonde. "And I think you're safe to go back to work, but if you don't mind, I'd like to drive you there and back until I feel comfortable the threat had been completely eliminated."

She was quiet for a minute and then nodded. "Okay, but I work nine to six. Aren't you sleeping at those times?"

"I can sleep when I'm dead," I deadpanned at her.

"Okay, deal," she replied, giggling.

God, this woman. She'd gotten under my skin in a matter of days and now the thought of spending even one day without her made my protective wolf come howling to the surface. I wouldn't live if anything happened to her. What she saw in me, I would never know. She thought I was her great wolf protector, but I was more like an avenging angel who would tear down the world if anyone laid a finger on her.

"Shit," I heard Shadow say.

I looked over to where he was staring and saw the two BSI agents walk through the front door. The male, Bishop, greeted Kovah with a fist-bump.

"Who are they?" Kalissa asked.

"Supernatural cops," I murmured.

She blinked big blue eyes up at me. "Huh? There's such a thing?"

"Yep, I'll explain later."

Viper and MyAnna approached the two agents. I followed them over. "What can we do for you?" Viper asked.

"We need to talk about a few things," Agent Bishop said. "Someplace quiet?"

Viper looked at his wife. "Hold down the fort?"

She leaned up and kissed him quickly. "You got it."

I looked down at Kalissa. "Stay here, okay? I'll be right back."

"Okay," she replied, looking a little frightened, and I hated that look. I wanted to tie her to my bed so she would always feel safe.

"It's all right, I'll just be next door. There are half a dozen vampires in here who know if anything happens to you, they'll have their fangs physically extracted by me personally."

She nodded. "Okay."

I kissed her on the forehead, and the other lieutenants, and I followed agents through the walkway and back into the clubhouse.

"What's up?" Viper asked when we finally had some quiet.

Agent Bishop pulled out his notepad and pen. "We understand you killed three humans on Sunday. Explain."

Shit. The BSI rarely got involved in our business as long as it was between us and other supes. What they could not and would not turn a blind eye to were when humans were hurt or killed by them. Good or bad, it was their job to make sure supes did not harm them.

"Self-preservation and self-defense, plain and simple," Viper replied, his arms folded across his cut.

"Exactly how?" Agent Shields asked as she typed into her phone.

"They killed three wolves, threatened to kill a human woman, and then kidnapped me," I supplied. "They were hunters. They weren't going to stop."

"Still," Agent Bishop said, "we have to open an investigation. I'll need to speak to the human girl, as well. Get her story."

"No," I said, holding up my phone. "I have her entire story recorded here. I won't have her traumatized again having to retell the murder of her boyfriend right before her eyes."

"I'll email you the audio file," Face said to Shields.

Agent Shields looked at Face then back at me. "Were you injured during your kidnapping?"

I nodded. "Yes, they stabbed me. Missed my femoral artery by centimeters."

"Do you have any documentation? Photos, emergency room paperwork?" she asked.

"Nope, had it sewed up privately. It's healed now." I flashed yellow eyes at her.

She did a double-take then typed something into her phone.

"Just out of curiosity, what were we supposed to do with these guys if not kill them? They were literally hunting us and the werewolves. Had already killed three wolves. You can go talk to Psycho," Phoenix said.

"The Bayou Wolves' leader? Yes, we will be doing that as well," Bishop said. "As for your question, the answer is call us. We would have taken care of them."

"How?" I asked, my hands on my hips.

Agent Shields looked at Bishop, then back to me. "We have them arrested and prosecuted in the regular way. They go to prison for murder."

"I find that hard to believe," Viper said. "They tell the jury they were killing werewolves and they'll be believed?"

"Let's just say some of the judicial process gets skipped in these cases, and I'm going to leave it at that," Bishop said, closing his notepad. "Now, I'd like to talk to the human girl."

"I already told you no," I said.

"We'll take the audio file as evidence, but it's literally our job to make sure she's all right."

I sighed. "Fine. I'll go get her."

Agent Shields's eyebrows went up. "She's here?"

I didn't answer her, I just headed toward Cobalt. No way were these cops going to interview her alone though. She'd been through enough.

23

INTERROGATION

Kalissa

I sat in Viper's office with two very serious-looking agents staring at me. The guy, Bishop, was tall with a spiky blond flattop and intense green eyes. His partner, Shields, had clear, olive skin and full lips. Her eyes were hard, though, like she'd seen too much in her young life.

"We've gotten the account of what happened to you on the night of September eighth, so out of courtesy, we won't ask you to repeat the story."

"Thank you," I said quietly. I took comfort in the fact that Harlan and Phoenix were standing outside the door. I didn't know these agents obviously, but they really hadn't given me a choice in speaking with them or not. "But, um, do I need an attorney or something?"

"No, you're not being charged with anything," Shields said. "We just want to make sure you feel safe here. You've been briefed on the world of the supernatural, yes?"

I nodded. "I found out Donny was a werewolf while we were dating. Since I know you're going to ask, he didn't tell me, I followed him one night."

"Quite the eye-opening experience, I'm sure that was," Bishop said, jotting on his notepad.

"That's an understatement," I murmured.

"And vampires. What has been your experience with them so far?" Bishop asked.

I shrugged. "Honestly, it's been uneventful. They aren't scary like I thought they'd be, and, aside from drinking blood from coffee cups and not going outside during the day, they seem like normal people."

"Nobody's threatened you or otherwise asked if they could 'feed' from you?" Shields asked.

"No, not at all."

"And how did you come to stay here instead of with the Bayou Wolves?" she asked.

I explained how they weren't properly protecting me. "Harlan told me to come stay here, that I'd be safer."

"The one they call Venom? You know he's a wolf, not a vampire, right?" Bishop asked.

"Yep, from the first day I met him. He never tried to pretend he wasn't. Honestly, I've never felt safer than when I'm with him."

"Yet, he managed to get himself kidnapped by humans," he replied.

I narrowed my eyes and felt defensive on Harlan's behalf. "And every day he kicks himself for letting his guard down. He was just out picking up pizza. They drugged him."

He nodded. "And what is your current relationship with Mr. Lahey?"

I wasn't sure how to answer that. "Um, sort of exploring a relationship I guess you can say?"

"You understand if you have children with him, they'll be werewolves. Correct?" Shields asked.

I put my hands up. "Hey, no need to hit the gas like that, lady. We're not even close to having that conversation so I'm not worried about it. But yes, I do know that about offspring. I don't think I even want children, anyway, so it's a moot point." I lifted my chin. It wasn't a lie, I really didn't know, mainly because of my current issue with food, I didn't think a pregnancy would be safe so I figured being a mom wouldn't ever be in the cards for me.

"Just wanted to make you aware," she said, typing into her phone.

"I appreciate your concern," I said dryly.

She looked me up and down. "Are they feeding you here?"

Oh, here we go. "Yes," I sighed and lowered my voice. "Look, I'll just cut straight to the point—I have an eating disorder. I'm working on it. Had it long before I met Harlan or even Donny."

Her eyebrows shot up. "Well, I'm sorry to hear that. I hope you can get healthy soon."

"Are we done?" I asked, already tired of these stupid questions. I get they had a job to do but I wasn't afraid or at risk being here with the Nighthawks. I'd never felt safer, especially when I was in Harlan's arms every night. My only complaint was their sleeping schedule. I had to keep to sleeping at night because I was going to go back to my day job soon. Every night, Harlan held me until I fell asleep and then stayed up all night with his club brothers. He came to bed as I was getting up in the morning.

"No, I have a few more questions."

"Okay…"

She looked me straight in the eye. "Who killed the Manchester brothers and Mr. Welch?"

I lifted a shoulder. "I don't know."

"You were there, weren't you? On Sunday when the vampires rescued Mr. Lahey?"

"Well, yes, but I was outside. I didn't really see anything—"

She cut me off. "But surely you heard them talking at some point. Which vampire killed which human?"

I gritted my teeth and told her honestly, "No, I didn't. I don't think you understand how secretive these guys are. Half the time they stop talking when I walk into the room. I would never dare ask what went on in that house. All I know is that the hunters were dead when the guys came out. I didn't ask how they died, nor if they were already dead when they got there, nor if they had killed them. And I don't want to know. By the way, the Bayou Wolves were there as well, just so you know." I sat back and folded my arms across my chest.

"So which of the Nighthawks, besides Mr. Lahey, were inside the house at the time of the murders?" Bishop asked.

"I don't remember," I lied. Definitely wasn't going to tell them that.

He stared at me hard for a few long, uncomfortable seconds, then jotted down more stuff.

"I gotta ask," I said, feeling brave, "what would you do to them if you knew precisely who killed whom? You can't exactly put vampires and werewolves in prison."

Bishop closed his notepad and slipped into the inside pocket of his suit jacket. "You're correct, not a human prison, anyway. We have our own lockup facility that's specially designed for supes."

My eyes widened. "Are you serious?"

Shields nodded and handed me a business card. "I want you to call either of us, day or night, if you need help, feel threatened, or otherwise just don't feel safe. Or, if you remember anything from that night that you wish to divulge. We will keep it discreet. Understand?"

I nodded and took the card. "Yes."

They both stood and exited through the door.

Venom came in and helped me stand. "You all right?"

"Yep, just fine. I suppose you want to know what they were asking me and stuff, huh?"

He grinned. "Nah, I heard it. We all did."

I stared at him in mortification and swallowed hard. "All of it?"

He put his arm around me. "Yes, all of it. You have nothing to be ashamed of or hide from me, Kalissa."

I nodded. "I know. I just hope you guys don't judge me. I'm working on my... problem."

He kissed the top of my head. "Honestly, I already suspected, but it's okay. I'll support you in any way I can."

Looking up at him, I asked, "You will? Donny used to just tell me to eat, used to get annoyed at me."

"I won't do that," he said, putting his hand on my cheek. "You've acknowledged your problem, that's the first step, right? We'll get through this together. And just know, I think you're sexy and beautiful the way you are. But if you put on some weight, I would love that as well." He kissed my nose.

I sagged in relief. Since things seemed to be getting serious between us, I was wondering how I would tell him about my stupid problem. Maybe I should make that appointment with Alice and see if she could help me. Harlan made me want to get better.

"Also, thank you for keeping quiet with the agents. I realize you don't know all the details, and we do that on purpose. Only the lieutenants and Viper know all the details when we go on these missions. It's to protect everyone else in the club—especially the old ladies. Just know, we don't ever expect you to get yourself into trouble for us. If you're ever backed into a corner, either by the cops or the bad guys, do what you need to protect yourself. We can handle any fallout. You understand?."

Nodding, I said, "Yes, and I appreciate it. You've all been so good to me, I would never do anything to betray any of you."

"It's not betrayal if handing out information could save your life. But in this instance"—he pointed to the office—"they're just the BSI. Their number one goal is to protect and shield humans. It's us they keep an eye on. They just wanted to make sure you weren't here under duress or being fed on or any of that nonsense."

"I knew they were just doing their jobs. They were a little intimidating at first, but they don't bother me."

"Good," he said. "Now, I'm hungry so I'm gonna go eat that burger Ally got for me that I'm sure is cold by now. But I'm happy to share it with you."

I shrugged one shoulder. "I could eat."

He beamed a sweet grin at me. "Awesome."

"Are you tired?" Harlan asked as he slowly stripped my clothes off. It was a nightly ritual we'd gotten into. He called it tucking me into bed. I called it him seducing me.

"A little," I replied as he peeled my leggings down my legs before I stepped out of them.

He grinned like the Cheshire Cat when he saw I had no panties on. So, while on his knees, he took full advantage by running kisses up my inner thigh. I shuddered, and once he got to the apex between my legs, he ran slow licks and kisses around my bare mound.

"Mmm," I moaned, slowly raking my fingernails through his hair. "More."

He used his fingers to spread my folds apart, and my legs widened as I stood, giving him better access. He used the tip of his tongue to lick and suck my sensitive bundle of nerves and I trembled even harder.

"Harlan," I groaned, tightening my grip on his hair.

He reached around and kneaded my ass cheek with his other hand as he continued to suck and lick between my folds. He moved his hand around to insert one finger into me.

"Oh, God!" I whimpered, shaking uncontrollably as a tidal wave of pleasure crested over me in a delicious climax that left me wanting to collapse. He continued to lick and suck in a delicious assault until I couldn't take any more. I pushed him away.

He picked me up and tossed me on the bed. I watched as he stripped all his clothes off, staring at me while I lay here, ready for him. I tore my shirt off over my head and threw it to the floor.

He grinned when he saw I wasn't wearing a bra. My breasts were so small I didn't see the point in wearing one most days.

He dove between my legs and kissed and sucked on me some more before running his lips up my stomach and to my breasts. His mouth fit over my whole right breast, and I groaned as he sucked and licked at the hardened peak.

I giggled and he looked up. "Enjoying yourself?" he asked.

"Your beard tickles."

"Good," he growled, moving to pay the other breast equal attention.

I was propped up on my elbows, watching him. When his cock probed me, my head craned back as he sucked harder on my nipple.

"Baby, please." I reached down to grab his hips.

"Tsk, tsk, tsk. So impatient for my cock, greedy little minx." He swirled his hips to tease my greedy hole some more, that piercing making me want more.

"Give it to me," I demanded, narrowing my eyes.

"So bossy." He chuckled but was still teasing me. He had his fingers tweaking both of my nipples. He licked his lips. "You want this cock, darlin'?"

"Yes," I moaned, my hips gyrating in need, trying to get him to put it in. I thought I was going to die if he didn't impale me immediately.

"Say it. Tell me you need it."

"Fuck me now, Harlan. Give me that huge cock. I wanna feel him inside me. I want that piercing rubbing me in all the right places."

With his eyes hooded with lust, he stared right into my eyes as he gripped both my hips and slammed into me, all the way to the hilt.

I cried out, gripping the sheets. "Oh, yes!"

He slowly pulled all the way back out. My eyes burst open, and I narrowed them at him in anger.

He chuckled. "Angry Kalissa is more like an angry kitten."

"No breaks," I snapped in mock anger.

"As you wish." He pushed back in and began to move slowly, pacing himself. He felt so damn good, so snug, like my pussy was made for his cock.

"Faster," I demanded.

"Yes, ma'am." He began to thrust faster and faster, chasing his release but making sure I got mine first. "Come for me, darlin'."

My hips moved in perfect rhythm with his as I gripped his shoulders and stared into his eyes, our breaths mingling, our hard pants mixed with the slapping of our bodies together.

"Shit! Oh, God!" I cried, that piercing hitting the exact right spot with eerie precision to make me dizzy with lust. My walls clamped around him hard, my nipples pebbling into hard little rocks.

Three more thrusts and he was done, squirting inside me while my whole body trembled along with his. He collapsed on top of me, my fingers still gripping his shoulders so hard they'd probably leave bruises.

"That," he said between breaths, "will never get old."

"Ditto," I breathed as he rolled off me. "Damn, Harlan. Your dick is like a magic wand, I never know what kind of tricks he'll play."

"Gotta keep you on your toes." He kissed my nose and pulled me to stand. "Now get your fine ass into the shower so I can wash you head to toe."

I giggled when he slapped my ass on the way to the bathroom.

24

LEGAL TROUBLES

Venom

I listened quietly as Andy explained things to the six of us. It had been over two weeks and we hadn't heard a peep from the BSI. Normally, that would be a good thing, but in this case, it just had us on edge.

"The problem is that I'm only familiar with regular criminal law. If I could get a set of statutes on the supernatural laws, I'd better be able to defend or otherwise represent you and the club properly," Andy said.

"You have a good point. If they're supposedly opening up a case on the Manchesters' and Welch's deaths, then we should be prepared for any charges they're going to throw down on us," Viper said.

"The BSI should supply to me, or at least tell me where I can access the laws so I can properly prepare a defense, if need be," Andy agreed.

I pulled the toothpick out of my mouth and looked around the empty club. Cobalt was set to open in an hour, so we had to make this meeting quick. "If you want my two cents, they may be a branch of the DOJ, but I find it hard to believe they have all kinds of legal statutes and bylaws they've put in writing. That would require them to file them at congress dot gov, where they'd be public information, and we all know they can't do that."

Andy nodded. "You're correct because I've checked there and there's nothing about supernatural anything. It's just Department of Justice laws and sentencing guidelines. And I searched for hours, even went in person to the federal courthouse downtown. They looked at me like I was crazy when I asked if they had any non-public information laws about supernatural crime. I risked going during the day too. Thank fuck it was cloudy and raining."

"Well, the bottom line is, they operate by their own rules and are a law unto themselves," Face said. "I also did a search and came up with nothing. The only things on the internet are videos and blogs by people who've claimed there's a secret government agency for supernaturals and they've had run-ins with them. And a bunch of fiction books with *X-Files* type stories in them."

"Not good," Viper said, shaking his head. "I mean, I've always sort of known that they operated by their own rules, but we've never really gotten on their bad side before, so I never worried about it. When we took out those hunters, I didn't think twice. They had to be dispatched quickly before they killed more wolves and then came after us next. I'm just pissed we couldn't get anything out of Eli before I took his head off. The BSI never once came to mind."

"I can talk to Nolan before I leave town," Kovah said. "Convince him and Shields to look the other way just this once."

"Right, because if we didn't technically break any federal laws, they're going to have to answer to my fancy new attorney," Viper said, smiling at Andy.

"Something tells me they won't give a shit about an attorney," I murmured, picking up my beer. "No offense." I grinned at the newcomer.

He waved a hand. "None taken, man."

"We'd appreciate it anyway, Kovah," Viper said.

"Where'd you get that name, anyway?" Andy asked Kovah. "What does it mean?"

He chuckled as he picked up a celery stick and dipped it in ranch dressing. "It's havoc spelled backwards with a K. I chose it when I had to reinvent myself. Real name's Dominic."

"Well, I never knew that," I commented.

"Me either," Phoenix and Face said in unison.

Kovah grinned behind his sunglasses. "Well, now ya do. And I think I'm gonna go back to using it when we get to New York. I'm old enough to have a grown son now, so I'll just get some new docs, say the old Dominic was my dad, since he's technically dead."

"Good idea," I said. "And try not to kill too many succubus... succubi up there."

His smile dropped. "No dice, bro. They all gotta die."

I put my hands up in mock surrender and bit back a smile. I loved getting a rise out of him. "Okay then, good luck."

Viper shook his head. "Back to the task at hand. I'm gonna call a meeting with the agents and see what they plan to do. I'm not going to get blindsided by some bullshit arrests. I need to plan a preemptive strike, keep a step ahead of them."

"I agree," Kovah said. "Just no harming the agents, especially Bishop. He's a good dude, solid, straight arrow. He's just doing his job."

"I know," Viper said. "I have no plans on harming them. I'm just not going quietly if they try to jam me or any of you up for this hunter business. I will not back down. You all dig?"

We all nodded.

"We got your six," Phoenix said. "Always."

"Always and forever," Shadow said.

After a long but uneventful night of just hanging out at Cobalt and discussing the legal problems some more, I was ready for bed. I looked at my watch to see it was time to wake up Kalissa for work. Over the past few weeks, she'd moved some of her stuff into the small apartment but wanted to keep her house. She owned it but still had a few years left to pay it off and we agreed it was a good investment to keep. The cat was temporarily living with her parents. If you thought cats hated wolves, you should see how they behaved around vampires. Downright psychotic and admittedly a little comical to watch. I offered to move into the house with her, but she said for the time being, she was still spooked and felt safer at the clubhouse, so I didn't argue.

I unlocked the apartment door and called out, "Good morning, sunshine." My smile dropped when I heard her vomiting in the bathroom. I quickly rushed in there to see her head damn near all the way in the toilet.

This wasn't the first time I'd caught her puking, but it was usually after a meal. Not always, though, as she'd made an agreement with me that she wouldn't do that anymore. That didn't mean that sometimes she had a weak moment and did it anyway. However, it had been a while since it had happened. Furthermore, she'd been asleep all night, not eating.

"Are you all right, darlin'?" I asked, holding back her hair.

She shook her head and there were tears streaming down her face. "No. Something's wrong." She weakly reached up and flushed the toilet.

I grabbed a washcloth and ran warm water on it before gently wiping her face. I sat next to her on the floor. "What do you mean? Did you eat something this morning?"

"No, that's why something's wrong. I didn't throw up on purpose. I just woke up a few minutes ago and felt overwhelmingly sick. There wasn't much to puke up though, mostly bile."

"Maybe you have a stomach virus? I forget humans get those sometimes."

She nodded. "Maybe. I better call into work just in case. I don't want to get anyone else sick."

"Good idea," I said, pulling my phone from my back pocket and handing it to her. I helped her stand and led her to the bed to sit.

After she made the call, I felt her forehead. "You seem a little warm, but I don't think you have a fever. Is there a thermometer in that medical kit you brought here?"

"Yes, but it's okay. I don't think I'm feverish. Just warm from throwing up. I'm gonna go back to bed, see if I feel better later."

I helped her under the covers and kissed her forehead before filling a glass of water and bringing it to her. "Drink."

She did as instructed and lay back down. I stripped down to nothing and crawled in bed with her, grateful werewolves didn't get stomach viruses. I held her as we both drifted off to sleep.

A few hours later, I was woken suddenly when I heard her throwing up again. I got out of bed and went to check on her.

"Just water, better than bile," she murmured as she swished out her mouth with another cup of water. "I hope this passes soon, because this sucks. I wonder where I got it from?"

"You literally work at a medical clinic. I'm sure some sick person breathed on you," I said.

"I need to be better about wearing my mask at work. I hate that thing."

I helped her back to bed, where she fell back to sleep fairly quickly. Sleep didn't come as fast for me, though. I was worried about her, so I just watched her sleep. She was already struggling with her weight and now this would probably set her back. I could only hope she'd be very hungry once the sickness passed and she was feeling back to normal again to get some food in her. Truth was, I was constantly worried about her health, but I could tell she genuinely was working on trying to eat more and get healthy. She even sometimes asked me to stay with her to stop her from going straight into the bathroom after a meal. I didn't really like having to do that, it felt too controlling, but I did as she asked. I drew the line at watching her use the toilet, though… I would have to just trust she was in the bathroom doing that and not purging.

I did eventually drift off, and when I woke at 4 p.m., she wasn't in bed. I threw some pants on, and when I realized she wasn't in the apartment, I opened the front door. I could hear her voice downstairs and breathed a sigh of relief.

After a quick shave and shower, I went downstairs to find her sitting in the breakroom with Jemini and Bloome. I kissed the top of her head. "How are you feeling?"

She smiled up at me as I went to the coffee pot and poured a mug full. "I'm still kinda nauseated but no more vomiting."

I stood with my butt against the counter as I sipped the coffee. "I'm going to order food to be delivered. Anything you're craving or you think would settle your stomach?"

She bit the side of her lip and said, "I really, really want spaghetti and meatballs."

I smiled. "Your wish is my command."

"And some chicken wings, extra spicy."

Now, I frowned. I knew she'd eat maybe five bites of spaghetti and be done, to which I would then finish it. No way she'd eat wings as well. But I wasn't going to discourage her. "You must be starving after all that throwing up."

She glanced at the girls, and a look I'd never seen before passed over her features.

I looked at Bloome, who was staring at her with her eyebrow cocked. "Go on," she said to Kalissa.

Kalissa looked at me sheepishly. "They think I need to take a pregnancy test."

My coffee mug froze at my lips and my eyebrows hit my hairline. "But you're on the pill. It's probably just a stomach bug."

"Pill's not a hundred percent," Jemini said, swiping on her phone and then showing me a photo of two babies who looked just alike. "Ask my cousin, these are her on-the-pill twins."

I, of course, knew absolutely nothing about pregnancy except how to make one. I swallowed hard and looked at my beautiful girlfriend. "What do you want to do?"

"I didn't want to tell you, but during all the chaos these past few weeks, I did forget to take my pill a few days. And a couple of days when I did, I had thrown up shortly after because I'd forgotten." She had tears in her eyes. "I'm sorry."

After setting the mug down, I walked over, made her stand, and put my fingers under her chin. "In no way do you owe me or anyone an apology. You're human and you've had your life turned upside down. Nobody can expect you to remember every little detail of everything. Now, let's go buy you a test. We'll go out to eat first, since we're both hungry. All right?"

Both girls sighed and smiled at us.

"You two, stop planning the baby shower in your heads. I already know you two are." I pointed at them both and narrowed my eyes in mock command.

"Guilty as charged," Jemini said, giggling.

"What's going on in here?" Shadow asked, his tall, imposing frame taking up the whole doorway.

"Kalissa's going to buy a pregnancy test," Bloome blurted.

Shadow's eyes widened and he said to me, "You got pups on the way already?"

Kalissa squeaked, her eyes wide. "Pups? Plural? Nobody told me you guys breed in litters!" Her breaths sped up like she was panicking.

"Thanks, you asshole," I said to Craig.

"I was just kidding, geez," he said. "It's only one pup."

Bloome set her coffee cup down and looked at him. "How do you know?"

He shrugged and grabbed a bag of blood from the fridge. "I can hear only one fast little heartbeat."

"Well," Bloome said, grinning from ear to ear, "guess you can save your money on a test." Then, she let out a squeal and clapped like she'd just won the lottery.

Jemini hugged her, then me. "Congratulations!"

"I need to sit down," Kalissa whimpered.

"I need a fucking drink," I murmured.

EPILOGUE

VOWS & VAMPIRES

Venom

One Month Later

My brother Robbie elbowed me in the ribs. "Getting married in a bar. Classy."

"Fuck off," I whispered as I tried to keep a smile plastered on my face.

Gabe stood beside me, also in a tuxedo, and covered up his laugh with a cough.

"You can fuck right off, too," I murmured.

"Shh. Here comes your bride," Gabe said.

My breath caught in my throat as I watched Kalissa walk into the Cobalt from the walkway between the bar and clubhouse. Her cream dress went all the way to her feet and flared out at the waist to accommodate her growing stomach. She was only three months along, but her belly poked out already due to how thin she already was. Thankfully, being pregnant with a baby wolf apparently caused a seriously voracious appetite, and all thoughts of her weight and wanting to stay thin went out the door. I couldn't feed her enough and there were no words to describe how happy that made me.

When I'd broken the news to my brothers, uncle, and cousins, they'd congratulated me and agreed to come down for the wedding. Robbie's wife sat next to Jordan, who brought his daughter Emmie with him. She was a beautiful fourteen-year-old with an infectious smile and a nonstop stream of dialogue. Unfortunately, things hadn't worked out between my brother and her mom, but he seemed to embrace being a dad. My uncle and aunt sat next to them, along with my cousins Aaron and Jeramy.

The news about the wedding and pregnancy had been easy to deliver to my family. What wasn't easy was explaining my situation. They'd thought I'd just been living here in New Orleans, working on the docks, not belonging to a motorcycle club of vampires. That took them a minute to accept. My brothers were pissed at me, but when I asked what vampires had ever done to them, they had nothing to say. I hoped by them meeting my friends—my brothers from other mothers—that they could see the side to them that I saw. That they weren't our "natural born enemies" and never would be.

The rest of the club members were in attendance, too, and I felt so grateful that they were here supporting us. My soul was happy and my heart was full at all the love and support Kalissa and I were receiving over our relationship and upcoming baby. I couldn't believe I was going to be a dad for the first time at forty, because I never thought it was in the cards for me. But I had never been happier. I was getting the family I always wanted but never knew I did. I vowed to myself and God that I would not turn out like my father and that I would love this kid with everything I had.

When Kalissa came to stand beside me, I recited the vows I'd written and meant every word of them. I slipped the two-carat diamond on her finger and knew she was it for me. She was my forever.

"I love you," I whispered against her lips before I kissed her for the first time since she became my wife a few seconds ago.

"I love you more," she replied after we broke the kiss.

The minister I'd hired introduced us as husband and wife, and a smile I couldn't control burst across my face when everyone I loved and cared for clapped and cheered for us.

The reception was held right here in the Cobalt Room, and I'd told the catering company to go heavy on the meats and proteins, knowing a lot of wolves would be in attendance. The wolves I wasn't expecting to see were Psycho and Demon as they came in and congratulated us.

Psycho grabbed Kalissa's hand and kissed the top of it. It looked ridiculously small in his humongous meat hook. "I'm glad you found another wolf to take care of ya. I'm really sorry again about Donny, but I know he would have wanted you to be happy."

Her eyes filled up with tears. "Thank you, Shep. That means a lot." She dabbed her eyes with a tissue she had tucked in her sleeve. "Damn pregnancy hormones."

Psycho's eyes went wide. "Y'all got a pup on the way?"

I nodded. "Sure do."

He shook my hand vigorously and smiled. "Congratulations!"

I bit back a smile. "Shep?"

He slid his gaze to Kalissa, then back to me. "Shepard, my legal name. Chicks hate using our club names."

"I know," I said, chuckling. "Harlan, nice to meet you."

"Send me a pic when that kid is born, I'll bring over some cigars. Got some good Cubans I've been savin'."

"Will do," I said. "Now help yourself to some food. Open bar too."

He clapped me on the shoulder. "Thanks, man."

Gabe came up behind me after Psycho and Demon walked off. "Who invited them?"

"I actually don't know," I said, feeling a little guilty that I hadn't.

"I did," Viper said. "I wanted them to see that Venom was taking good care of Kalissa."

"Thanks, man," I said.

Viper hugged Kalissa. "Congratulations, little lady. You're a beautiful bride."

"Thanks," she replied, a beautiful pink flush stealing the pale from her cheeks.

"I helped with the dress and hair," MyAnna commented.

"She did," Kalissa agreed. "I've been so fortunate to have so much help with everything in such a short amount of time. Between working, throwing up, and eating my weight in chicken wings, I've been busy."

We all laughed.

I pulled Viper aside. "You know, it's been weeks. No word from the BSI?"

Viper nodded. "I heard from them. We'll discuss it later, though. Now's not the time."

He was right. "Fine, but I'll be by tomorrow to get the scoop."

He chuckled. "Okay. But you really should take a honeymoon before that baby comes."

"She's too sick. She's afraid any long car or plane ride would make her feel worse," I said.

"That's understandable."

"You guys going to stay here?" he asked, inclining his head toward the clubhouse.

"I don't think so. I doubt you guys want to listen to a crying baby all hours of the day and night. We'll move into her house for the time being."

"The girls will be very disappointed. That kid is gonna have like four aunties," he joked.

"And a lot of uncles," Gabe said as he approached.

"Wouldn't have it any other way."

After the wedding, and after my family had gone to their respective hotels, Kalissa and I crawled into bed in the apartment. I propped my head up on my hand and used my other to rub over her hard little stomach bump.

"Thank you for having my baby. I'm sorry he's making you so

sick. I wish I could take some of it on for you."

She smiled up at me and rubbed her thumb over my chin, running it through my beard. "Supposedly, it only lasts three months so maybe it'll stop soon. Also, how do you know it's a boy?"

"I don't think any men in my family can make girls. They've all tried. They just kept coming out with extra parts."

She laughed. "Your cousin has a girl. She's beautiful."

"That's true," I agreed. "Forgot about that. Maybe there's hope for a girl yet."

"Is that what you want?" she asked, piercing me with those incredible baby blues.

"I honestly don't care, as long as it's healthy and strong."

She leaned up and kissed me. "I agree. Are we naming it Harlan if it's a boy?"

I frowned. "No. It was my father's name, and he was a bastard. I'd rather find something else."

"Whatever you want," she whispered, kissing me while pushing me on my back and peppering kisses all over my face as she straddled on my stomach.

"You're so damn beautiful, you know that?" I said, running my hands up her waist and around her to ass.

"I hope you still think so when I'm a beached whale." She smiled but it didn't quite reach her eyes.

"Hey," I said. "You're going to be even more beautiful when your belly's big and swollen with my child. Then, after it's born, you'll be a hot MILF."

She smiled down at me. "Thank you for loving me just the way I am."

"Always," I whispered, pulling her head down so I could kiss my gorgeous bride and show her without words how I'd never let her go.

THE END

NIGHTHAWKS MC SERIES

Viper

Shadow

Phoenix

Venom

Face

ABOUT THE AUTHOR

C.J. is a USA Today bestselling author living in Colorado but wishes she was someplace warmer. She loves the SF 49ers and has a weakness for expensive shoes. She's the author of over 40 novels and short stories that contain both fantasy and paranormal romance with kickass heroines and strong alphas. Having recently retired from a twenty-year career in federal law enforcement, she's looking forward to the next chapter in life.

She can be found on Facebook, Instagram, and on her website, cjpinard.com.

PINARD HOUSE
PUBLISHING

Use your device's QR code reader to get a link to all of C.J.'s books!

Made in the USA
Middletown, DE
11 July 2022